Montauk

The Disappearances

By

Richard Prince

authorHOUSE®

AuthorHouse™
1663 Liberty Drive, Suite 200
Bloomington, IN 47403
www.authorhouse.com
Phone: 1-800-839-8640

First published by AuthorHouse 11/9/2007

ISBN: 978-1-4343-2255-5 (sc)

Library of Congress Control Number: 2007904635

Printed in the United States of America
Bloomington, Indiana

This book is printed on acid-free paper.

ACKNOWLEGDEMENTS

My book was possible because of many wonderful people. I particularly thank my wife, Linda, who supported me with just the right mixture of good humor, bright ideas, patience and love.

I am extremely grateful to my brother Kenneth Prince for his clever plot insight and to his late wife, Margaret Lewis Prince, whose wonderful wit and humor are sorely missed. I thank my mother and father for their encouragement and faith in my perseverance and dedication to my project. I am deeply indebted to Eugenia Bartell, my editor extraordinaire, for her time and valuable advice. Her belief in my story sustained me throughout its writing; her encouragement will make this book a success. A special thanks to Eddie Di Roma for his time consuming help; keeping me going in the right direction. I owe special thanks to

Steve Lubell for his invaluable assistance, his investigative knowledge and technical support. I would also like to acknowledge the grateful help I received from Dottie De Misco who gave me my first start, Wilton Kelley, my business partner, Mike from the Amagansett Fish Market, Paul from Atlantic Liquors, Gary and Judy Hall, Bob and Helen Admundsen, my father in law, NYPD Inspector, Retired, Richard Di Roma, Jack Yee, Joe Demarco, Richard Janis, Manager of the Star Island Yacht Club and Steve Deal for his excellent technical support. I especially thank the late Christopher and John Pfund, never to be forgotten, for their insight into the young Montauk fleet's beginning and their tireless help and support, day and night, which ensured that the fleet would be ready to sail at first light.

PROLOGUE

An unthinkable sense of impending doom is lurking in this hamlet. It cannot be stopped. Montauk has many personalities; she is a non-forgiving paradise. Drop your guard and this old salt known as "the gray lady" will show you no mercy, no exceptions. She's been here too long and has seen it all. Just count the number of ship wrecks along her northern and southern coasts. Even Captain Kidd was done in by this seemingly enchanting old lady. This coastal site is the shifting grounds of virgin dunes, pristine safe harbors and jetties. It's the surf roaring to the south and the quiet bays humming to the north.

Montauk is one of the great surfcasting ports on earth. People from all over the world come here to try their luck. It's a Mecca, a calling, a luring to the anglers seeking out the most exciting and heart pounding striped bass and blue fishing ever.

This quaint old village, where for many generations, its hardy men and women have earned a livelihood by netting and fishing the depths of her deep waters and shallow bays, has been rewarding. Her fishing grounds both in the Atlantic and in the bays are the finest in northern and southern waters. Here marine life is found in abundant crop numbers as well as countless game fish and shell life. Numerous loves have met their fate along these scenic shores. She has a charm but then there is her dark side hidden by her remarkable warm and seductive nature. Strangely enough, even a few surf casters, with their keen sense of adventure and intuitive knowledge of her beaches have perished.

Chapter 1

It was sun up and to the east the red ball arose and radiated like a furnace, its rays warming the very soul of a Montauk fisherman, standing on a rock in his wet/dry suit. Todd Miller was exhausted from the strong September wind. A limber man, with the body of an acrobat, nimble and in the full vigor of his early forties, stood erect, occasionally brushing back a forelock of yellow hair and searched the water for activity through eyes as gray as a seagull's wing. Todd was perched on a rock known to the locals as tabletop.

The unrelenting surge from the sea and wind drove human spirit to simplicity; catch or be damned. All of one's skills must be honed. The next cast could produce a thirty or forty or even a fifty pound striped bass known as a cow. She was the breeder of future generations: only the best fish under the light. Fishing on one's own is testing the limit. One slip could put you in harm's way. A rogue wave from out of the sea can slam the best of fishermen down and pull him into the abyss.

Although Todd was a bright veteran, he never lost sight of the dangers lurking under his feet. Todd remembered his old guru's words of wisdom, "If it can happen it will" and "if you have the least doubt, don't engage". Damn, Todd loved Clive like a father. Standing on tabletop, Todd let his mind wander and thought of the day he first met Clive. He and his friend Billy, one of the local sharpies, had just finished fishing the out going when Clive pulled up and exited his truck. "How's the fishin', Bubb?" he asked Billy, not showing Todd any recognition. Billy, of Irish descent, with a lean frame, was strong as a battling blue. His face was tattered with a reddish beard that matched his hair and his age was beginning to show. He was a master carpenter and a fishing guide who had taught Todd all he knew about fishing. Yet, Todd was awe-struck meeting Clive for the first time. He knew he was standing before one of Montauk's legends.

Clive, of Norwegian heritage, was a striking man, over 6'3", with sandy colored hair and deep amber eyes as penetrating as a tiger's on the hunt. His body was strong like an athlete's. Todd would never forget when

Clive saved his life, shortly after they first met. To this day the experience haunted Todd's thoughts as he recalled how Clive's hands gripped him like a vise as a rogue wave tore him off his footing. Todd knew he had escaped a fisherman's worse nightmare when, as he was tumbling out of control into a dark pounding sea with a fully loaded waist band, Clive had saved him. The two became genuine friends and fishing buddies.

Todd's three hour ritual of fishing from 2:00am to 5:00am was over. He eased himself carefully west off the rocks, planted his feet firmly in the sand and felt safe from another night under the Light. "Lots of reminiscing but no keepers to take home to Jamie," he said to himself. "No problem, some nights the fish win and at home I've half a freezer packed for the winter and I still have eight weeks to fill it, God willing. One day I'll be too old for this routine. Oh well, not looking forward to that, enjoy it while I can." He arrived at his truck, hopped in and after awhile the heat kicked in, warming his body and relaxing his muscles.

Down at Jack's coffee house the night crew began to show up. Jack's a local hangout, had the best coffee in town; steaming hot and strong which their bones welcomed. They didn't have to order. Jack knew their breakfast patterns. All the talk was about fishing part truths, part lies, all were in the mix. They all knew each other and they knew how to interpret the facts from the fantasies. It was a good way to start the mornings.

Everything about Jack's appearance was pretty average. His hair was a medium brown; he was not too tall or too short and had a fair build. He smiled constantly, talked a lot and was extremely warm and courteous. In fact, he was so friendly that one had to wonder why. Oh well, business was business and Jack was Jack.

He had just finished pouring Todd's coffee as Todd walked through the doorway. Heads turned at the sound of the door bells. Their jingling sent anxious anticipation as soon as someone entered the café. Jack was the first to ask, "Any keepers?" Todd shook his head and explained how quiet it was; no bait, no birds, just a few shorts for the effort. Jack announced, "Harley, here, picked a twenty pounder and Kelly two, one sixteen pounds, one eighteen and Wilton is high hook for the day with a twenty seven pounder."

Now Montauk is filled with enigmas but all know never to break the rule. Never ask, "where or what on". It was one of the local traditions not known to the rest of the world. Montauk was self contained and disliked outsiders. Yet, information was rarely shared and secret fishing grounds were kept sacred sanctuaries as were the lures that produced the cows.

Not only did Jack own the coffee house but he took pride in keeping a log of the day's catch. The locals would come in to find out what was going on. This helped Jack, not a fisherman, to feel he was one of the guys. When Todd finished his second cup of coffee he stood up and put nine dollars on the counter. Jack handed him his family's breakfast in a hot bag designed to keep the eats warm until Todd got home.

Todd hopped into his truck and moved off down Main Street. He turned right on Second House Road, continued for about a mile, made a left on Navy Road and at the end turned right on to his private road. A minute later he arrived at his house which sat on a cliff overlooking Fort Pond. Looking west one could see New London, Connecticut and to the northeast Culloden Point, named after the English ship, Man of War, that sunk during a gale, losing all hands. To the east rose the Montauk Water Tower, The Montauk Manor, Duryea's and Rough Riders. Between Culloden Point and Rough Riders, on the opposite shore, quaint houses dotted the hillside.

Todd's house was white brick with a black mansard roof and surrounded by scrub oak. He entered his home through the dining room and placed the breakfast on the table which had been set by Jamie the night before. There was a routine in the Miller family which kept the peace. Views from the dining room, family room and the master bedroom were worth every penny that Todd had out into the house.

As he went into the children's bedrooms, Todd, Jr., five years old and Nancy, six years old were already stirring to begin their day. Todd kissed them good morning; they knew their morning ritual. Entering the master bedroom, Todd knelt down and kissed Jamie, as she threw her arms around him, "Any keepers?" she asked. He told her it was quiet and handed her a cup of coffee. With breakfast over, the rumbling yellow school bus arrived right on time. Nancy and Todd, Jr. took their assigned seats. The bus continued on its way to the Montauk Elementary School. Their Mom followed. She was the fifth grade teacher. Todd waved as Jamie pulled out of the driveway.

He cleaned up the dishes, lit his pipe and looked out upon the water contemplating what might be swimming underneath. Fishing was foremost on his mind. It was a way of life in Montauk. Shortly, he awoke from his daydreaming and left for work. Todd was the owner of the Montauk Liquor Store. As soon as he arrived he turned on the lights, music and his

VHF radio, settled down at his desk to pay some bills and waited for his first customer.

Chapter 2

The "Shark Killer, II" was captained by one Calvin Cain. Captain Cane, a hardy strong willed man, now forty five, had reduced his life to a simple purpose; catch, sell, get rich and retire. He always overcompensated with his fishing line, hooks, tackle, etc. A lost fish is a worthless fish. Anchorage, fuel, bait, equipment and boat expenses were on the rise and there was "no sense putting in the effort and losing a fish because of faulty equipment or poor seamanship," he was known to say. He checked everything the night before as thoroughly as a mountain climber would do before going aloft. Calvin would never be the laughing stock of the Montauk fleet. He had his pride like all the others. When a boat chopped through the harbor after a long day of fishing and then did not check into the weighing station its Captain became the gossip of the Montauk Captains' Association. Calvin swore to himself he would never be a part of that buzz. His motto was, "never to leave a trophy behind" and he didn't. He loved the sea and had a deadly dedication to fishing.

Calvin was a most frugal man and never wasted a penny. He was six feet tall and his unusual large one eye was as dark as a shark's; no shine, just a deep dark dull stare. When looking into that eye you saw a man of non-forgiving evil; no emotion, just blunt complacency like a great white on your first dive. He lost his left eye eight years ago on the stern of his boat while pulling in a small mako shark. The line was an eighty pound test Dacron, with a cable leader that was attached to a 12/0 hook. The hook tore out of the shark's mouth when she went into her violent, thrashing deadly dance. Calvin knew instantly it was lights out for his left eye when he felt the pierce of the hook.

Now viewing the black patch on his left eye in the mirror his spine tingled, his face clenched. He knew how Ahab felt about the whale and thought, "One day I'll have my revenge." Calvin had a body of a weight lifter and forearms that made Popeye's look meek. His black curly hair was tied in a pony tail hanging down to his shoulders. His mustache was short but his wavy beard reached his chest. He could have passed for one of Leif Erikson's Viking warriors. Calvin was dressed always in off shore gear down to his boots, like a fireman, ever ready for the sound of the bells. If the fish were in, the "Shark Killer, II" would begin to hunt.

Calvin had a calm disposition on the outside but that could turn at the drop of a hat. Unlike his bother, Nathan, in a three piece suit, the Administrator of the Montauk Rehab and Nursing Center, Calvin was the master of the sea, or so he thought. Their parents established the center in 1956 and hoped both sons would follow in their occupation. But Calvin had other dreams since the day his father had taken him fishing at age sixteen; the eldest son by two years. They went out on the charter boat, "Blue Jewel" named for blue fin tuna. Right away Calvin realized his course in life. No bed pans for him. To hell with his parents and even now with his parents deceased, he felt that his brother Nathan could just sit in his oak office and cajole young folk who wanted to rid themselves of their Moms and Dads. He would rather be at the canyon seventy or so miles out in the ocean, fighting a trophy fish for five hours than spend a minute with those misdeeded, self seeking, ungodly people. These were the people whose parents had brought them into the world, nurtured them, cried and smiled with them. They did their best and tried to provide for all their worldly needs. This, notwithstanding, they would drop them in Nathan's center, make arrangements for the rest of their lives and leave not feeling a pang of guilt. "We are so busy, we have no time for them," they wailed. Maybe they should have check with the Asians. "What's a Rehab Center, what's a Nursing Home?" they would ask; only in America! Oh well, free of Mom or Dad or both it was time to party.

Calvin hated those phonies and thought they should be thrown to the sharks. Nathan, on the other hand, offered the kids the easy way out. Years of experience enlightened him as to what buttons to push. He was a smooth talker and got right to the point. Nathan knew the ins and outs of spinning his web around the unsuspecting prey while they chatted aimlessly about their concerns. He knew when to come in for the kill, sign the deal and warmly confide in them as he pushed them out the door. He was the perfect mortician, always in black or gray or navy. No one noticed or cared. He held all the aces. He knew he was "their out". Nathan made it a practice never to let them feel the slightest pang of remorse. He warmed them and comforted them at the same time. He would see to all their needs. Nathan, always took them on a tour; the final "coup de grace". It never failed; another signed agreement, more government money. He often sighed, "What a life! It's almost too easy!" The thread of commonality between the brothers was that they knew what bait to use to get the job done.

Calvin was the ultimate testimony to the elusive and ever wistful treasure known as the "Montauk Dream". He was a small businessman trying to stay out of the red. His only mate was his sometime friend, almost girlfriend, Cary. She was no winner but she was not a loser. She could do it all and that's what kept Calvin and Cary pretty much together. Her father, Captain Richard, taught her all she knew about the sea on his charter boat, "The Princess II". Calvin and Cary shared a passion for fishing. Love was at the ebb tide. Both understood and neither gave a damn; fish hard and fish good; that's really all that mattered to both. They had met at Salador's one morning at breakfast and ten years later their bumpy relationship continued. Their hate or almost love dependence was still in tact; he master, she mate. Oh well, that's the nature of Montauk. You never know what's up from one day to the next. Tomorrow could bring a blue bird of a day or the danger of a nor'easter.

Montauk has a large population of Irish, Scottish and Dutch descendants. Cary was a mixture of all three. She could hold her own in any argument. At five feet, eight inches, one hundred and fifty pounds, she could do battle with the best. As an excellent helmswoman she knew Calvin's thoughts well and had learned to anticipate his plans before he would yell up his orders. "Damn that man, I so could hate him," she often thought, but, there was, at times, his real soft side. This was a rough and competitive business and it made you hard and even downright ruthless. Their relationship was bonded by big fish, big money and the thrill of fishing. What a life until the fish went south!

Cary had kind green eyes and somewhat of a pretty face for an old fishing salt at age forty one. Her once youthful skin had taken a toll from the elements. Fishing open waters under the sun over the years creeps up on a person. Nature is unrelenting to the frail human body. Enough is enough. The body matures more rapidly exposed to the sea. Her once golden hair, now a striking gray, was worn in a bun, to keep it safe from the day's dangers. She, too, wore off shore weather gear, even to church. Calvin was adamant about always being prepared; the call could come at any moment.

Cary was well known in the fishing village as Calvin's mate and all respected and liked her down to earth personality. She had an unusual sense of humor and could captivate you with her thrilling fishing stories. The old timers loved talking to her and getting a glimpse into the reclusive world of Calvin Cain. Thereafter, the gossip would flow throughout the hamlet. Cary looked the part of a sad sack but she loved life. And, yes, she thanked the Lord for Calvin. She was her own woman but she had found her man. She thought one day this would all end; it was inevitable. Perhaps they would settle down in her small cottage off Culloden Point; only ten more mortgage payments until it would be hers outright. She never told Calvin about the cottage. It would be a surprise. They could watch the sun lower itself over Gardiner's Bay, tilting their wine glasses and light a fire. "Nice dream," she muttered to herself, fingers crossed.

Chapter 3

Big game fish was Calvin's meat. His quarry included but was not limited to: mako, blue shard, hammerhead dusky, thresher, tiger, porbeagle, sandshard, the majestic broadbill swordfish, dolphin, white marlin and blue and yellow fin tuna. These were the big bucks fish. For his own amusement he caught squid, sea bass, flounder, blackfish, weak fish, porgy, pollock, striped bass, fluke, mackerel, bonita, cod, bluefish and he even had a taste for sting rays and skates. Calvin knew how to play the game. He was a non conformer and didn't play by the rules. He was a gamekeeper not a sportsman. You took his bait and you were dead history; all that sort of thing. That's the nature of Montauk. Be smart or be outsmarted.

Calvin and Cary were doing extremely well through the summer season as were some of the other boats.

They all had their secrets. The Captains had their pride and reputations to keep up. Calvin did not advertise or want customers since Cary and he were only interested in the meat; the big fish and all the money they shared. Just the two of them extracting thousands of pounds of fish each week was fine. There appeared to be no end to the hunt. The money was good; the bills were paid. All in all this was a banner year! Calvin drove Cary hard but he knew her breaking points as well as his own. The season would be coming to a close in a few months now that it was September. The winter layover would be rest enough until another season. But now it was bite the bullet time and they both understood the game and the pay was gold. No one complained and no one gave a damn if you did; one Captain, one mate, one boat. You fished hard during the day, took the bumps as they came and welcomed the night's rest. That's the way it was for generations of fishermen and that's the way it would continue to be. You knew what you were getting into when you chose this occupation just as you knew of the rewards at the end of a good day.

Calvin loved being his own master; Lord and Captain. He was fascinated with the sea, the breeze, the sun ups and the sun downs. He was one with the elements and had no regrets with his path in life. He escaped the doldrums of work; every day brought a new enigma to tease his wit. Calvin was up too the challenge and with Cary on board things worked always to his advantage.

The "Shark Killer II" worked tirelessly but had fits of fatigue needing fine tuning and daily inspections. She was a down eastern; length thirty eight feet, beam twelve feet. Penny for penny she proved her worth in a gale. Her keel was designed to cut smoothly through the "groans of roaring wind, rain and sea," as an old seafarer once said. Powered by her Yanmar diesel engine she could do twenty five knots. An extremely economical craft, she, nevertheless, sported two color fish finders, two VHF radios, JRD radar, Furuno GPS, two wash down pumps, a head with a macerator, over an eighty gallon fuel tank and an aluminum frame with white and green trimmed windows all around. She slept four passengers comfortably, was equipped with a kitchen area and had a TV and stereo. There was even more to her but Calvin never let on as to what new wriggles he added. Her designers built her to be un-burdensome; easy-going, easy-sailing and easy-running.

No matter your "sea of trouble" the down eastern would eventually and effortlessly ease her way back to port. Calvin was well aware of his obligation to her and never fell short of his duties. There was a trustworthiness between master and boat that was unspoken. All in all she was a very sturdy, dry, safe craft that you could depend upon out in the cold, blue Atlantic. Out fifty, sixty or seventy miles your life relied upon her overall workability. Calvin made damn sure she was seaworthy.

The boat was priority one and she got Calvin's daily attention. She and she alone made it possible to pursue the meat. She also took a chunk of Calvin's money which he resented since he was a frugal man by nature and was pissed when he had to shell out to refit and replace items and fuel up and re-bait. Prices were on the rise to his dismay which made him even crankier. "Damn those bastards. How the hell is one to make a living at these inflated prices?" he often repeated. "The market isn't keeping up to the hike, in fact, some of the meat prices are going down due to the banner year we're enjoying. Screw the government, screw the fishmongers and screw the business community. They're all leeches," he ranted, "sucking my hard earned money."

Cary knew to stay clear of him when these tirades took place. Calvin would get over it once they were out in open water. He believed in himself and that was all. He, being a righteous man, would damn all else. Hope, he felt, was for those sorry asses, who had to depend on those charts that indicated good fishing grounds and their fish finders. What a miserable bunch these bastards were according to him. And they call themselves fishermen? Really, they sure were in deep shit when their electronics failed or they lost their charts. Like all boats, Calvin had the same gear, but used it sparingly. He relied on his wit, experience and bait.

Calvin had been experimenting with a new secret bait. He marinated his bait overnight in a mixture of porpoise and shark blood. In theory, this would make it more aromatic and rancid, perking the interest of the meat. He liked it and thought they would, too. As his trial experiment proved successful, the production was great. Things could not have gone better. The fishmongers were happy and the money was good. This did not go unnoticed by the others and Calvin knew he was the buzz of the fishermen. Of course, because he was so covert about his experiment, no one could imagine what he was up to, not even his mate, Cary.

At first, Cary thought it was just a good run of luck. Knowing Calvin in the way she did, she suspected he was up to something what with that new set of fifty five gallon drums outfitted with a hand pump and six inch, ten foot long hoses. Better not ask, she thought, and wait it out until he clues me in. He always did, in time. He was forever tinkering with some new widget or gadget; some new fish catching toy. "Whatever he's up to, it's paying off big time and the bottom line is that's all that counts, especially for me being his mate. My mortgage payments are down and soon the cottage will be mine," she whispered happily to herself. Cary couldn't recall any of his concoctions failing. She liked that in him; always full of ideas and secrets, a cut above the others. She smiled to herself, "What the hell did he hatch this time? Oh well, I'll know one of these trips. Keep your eyes forward, helmswoman, before that "eye" notices my staring curiosity and lashes out with one of his ungodly roars."

Calvin looked every part of a contender but behind that black patch was a worth of knowledge devoted to the slaying of fish. His delivery system was simple as were most of his trumped up gadgets; pump out the chum and wait. Calvin knew better than to trust Cary with his latest device. After all, Cary was close to her brother, Liam, who chartered the "Breathless II". Calvin felt she would as usual pass on to Liam any new wriggle of his. That's what brothers and sisters do. Before long the whole fucking fleet would know and Calvin made damn sure he kept his business to himself. Never once did they offer him any advice and he remembered when he was starting out his questions fell on deaf ears. It was a hard way to learn this lesson but he also learned not to ever reveal his knowledge. Calvin didn't brood over this but he wondered how he could read their minds. True, he was learning their ways, but he needed more. That's life in Montauk; everybody had a whisper in the ear attitude. "Screw'em," he yelled. "Soon I'll cut through their childish bullshit of 'sotto voce'. They think they closed the door on me but session one is not over yet, boys."

Chapter 4

Calvin was not a gambler by nature; however, court-ing danger was not new to him. He was aware of the risks and knew there was no defense to his tact if he got caught. A risk taker he was and that made him, in his mind, a man of the sea. Now, he had to take the chance and do what he must do. "Damn it," he thought "this new wriggle is designed to put me on an even par with those guys."

He set his plan in motion one moonless night pre-setting his watch alarm for 3:00am. If all went accord-ing to plan he would have six hours in which to do his work. Dressed all in black to blend in with the shad-ows around the dock and armed with only a flashlight, pen and pad, he proceeded to his first target, ever vigi-lant of people activity.

Boarding the "Queen of Ages II" by climbing up the aft ladder he walked directly to the wheelhouse door. As he suspected, it was not locked. An easy entry and once inside he closed the door and scanned the docks again. "Good, no activity, all going accordingly," he said to himself. His next move was to find it. He ruffled through drawers; nothing .This he did not plan on. "Did they take it home with them?" he questioned. "Probably, it's worth its weight in gold, shit," he answered himself.

Calvin was searching for a collective history of the boat's offshore fishing agenda. His heart started pounding with his disappointment. "Why, oh why, are the God's against me, this was suppose to be so simple," he anguished. Turning and shining his light on the Captain's chart table, he was transfixed by what the light disclosed. There it was, in all its splendor; a blue, leather bound Captain's log! He could barely control himself. His fingers, a bit shaky, touched and stroked the book. He felt as if he was about to enter someone's mind. The history of the boat and its secrets, yes, its offshore mystery's, that no one would share, was now, his. "Now I'll know, you bastards, now I'll know," he cried.

He grabbed the log and sat on the cold iron floor. Comfort was the last thing on his mind. He opened the journal eagerly and read and read and read. He filled his note pad with all the treasures the log divulged. When he finished he replaced it and went to his next task.

Calvin boarded the "Blue Ocean I." Again all went according to plan. He found the log tucked in a leather bag next to the Captain's chair. He took notes and left. That night he accomplished his goals on all five boats. What a wealth of knowledge; years of information! "No wonder," he thought, "no one would share. This is their livelihood, oh well, it's mine, too. Screw those bastards, those hard nosed, self indulging drunks. Now I have their precious thoughts," he continued spitting. "I have their history and by the power of the sea I'll fry their asses. Ultimately, I'll be the best," Calvin announced to no one.

During the moonless week, Calvin climbed on fifteen more boats; a total of twenty boats had he entered and left; all unsuspected by the owners. It could be said that he was a devious man but weren't they? When Calvin returned to his boat after the last log was read, he sat on his mattress, in his master bedroom, gloating. In his mind there existed a state of war and he had just won the decisive battle. He took the offense and was victorious. His sneak attack paid off big time. This intelligence gathering was a wondrous worth of offshore information that he would analyze. He was now on even ground with all of them. "Let the best man be left standing," he exclaimed proudly.

The thrill of it left him tingling; he had to kick himself back to reality. He perused his notes with an utmost respect and awe. The notes were hard earned knowledge fought for over a lot of time. Now it was as if he was entering the past through the present. One by one they had cracked the code. Calvin held their tenacity in the highest reverence and developed a new respect for their way of life giving him a new attitude toward the brotherhood of those weathered beaten faces. They were, after all, true sea dogs, knew the risks and loved their families. He felt a little discomfort; almost ashamed of his behavior. "Shit, why didn't they take me into their confidence? Damn, does it always have to be this way? That's Montauk, 'sotto voco' rules," Calvin remembered. He went through his notes over and over and over. Then he saw it. There was a pattern emerging.

The skippers used various methods of hunting down their trophies, each adding his or her little twist or improvement as they saw fit. Angling, you know, is not an exact science. It's trial and error. Ask Mundus, Calvin smiled. Inwardly there's a high-sea maverick who cooked up a lot of shit! Calvin patiently pieced together the puzzle by correlating the several bits of information from the different log books. He organized and proceeded to put two and two together. The work was grinding, like cutting through a brick. Cal pushed on, feeling the end result, would surely be worth his efforts. He chuckled to no one in particular, "Why, hell, all those awful trials and errors I shall avoid, thanks to these Skippers." And so began his outline:

1. *Use three rigs at different levels; this approach allows the baited rigs to use different water temperatures and currents, thereby taking advantage of the different species cruising in the water's depth.*

2. *Rust your hook in Clorox overnight to camouflage them in the bait.*

3. *Be ever aware of surface feeding fish and birds circling high above or near the horizon diving at the water. Keep an eye out for seaweed and other debris floating on the surface; this could be a producer of hiding fish. These gamesters take advantage of any structure.*

4. *Game fish have their hook-up rules; direct fast pickup by a voracious attack on the bait or a toying approach. Either way they accept or reject the goodies that are offered. The very slow mouthing tactic is for the critter to hold the bait in his mouth scenting it but not accepting it; then release; then their*

disappearance. Sometimes you have to tease the combatants. (Calvin thought there must be other variations and planned to experiment with the old hard knocks approach.).

5. *Big fish love structure; a rocky bottom compared to a flat sea floor. Rocks provide a haven for fish on which they feed. Big gamesters prefer drop offs; a place where the sea floor drops abruptly to deep water.*

6. *When you're on a drift, judge how the wind and currents are affecting your ship's movements.*

7. *Conditions change from day to day. Check food availability, water temperatures. Barren areas could change to infested areas the very next day.*

8. *Their logs indicated the use of kite flying techniques to catch combatants or the use of crossbows. (Calvin considered this method with a little apprehension but would tuck it away for possible experimentation.)*

9. *Most big game love pilot whale meat. Its scent is irresistible. Whiting is another tasty dish to offer. Bunker chum was third on their list.*

10. *Live bait is superior to all other forms of bait, but depending upon conditions, this is not necessarily the golden rule.*

11. *Always set your chum slick upwind. It's been proven to yield the best results.*

12. *After a big game hook-up toss your flag buoy to mark your chum line beginning.*

13. *Hooking success was the greatest downwind for tagging the roving creatures. Down currents gave more realistic movement to dead bait. The scent carried more of an appetizing lure to the big fellow's nose. Flat, calm conditions produced less fish. However, on the other hand, windy conditions agitated the bait to look lively and lured a big fish for the strike.*

14. *Temperatures influence a fish's dining habits. At lower degrees fish appeared to have no appetite for live or fresh bait. However, at higher temperatures they became gluttonous; their digestive enzymes turned them into cud-chewing diners.*

15. *Big bait fish are not turned on by small snacks. They preferred the flavor of longer strips of fillet, the narrower the better.*

16. *They seemed to be in agreement that number 12/0 single wire leader worked best at eighteen to twenty inches long. They all chose tobacco colored leader. It appeared indestructible; not developing weak links.*

17. To give the bait the appearance of a waving tail, they cut their bait four inches wide and at a thickness of three inches.

18. They all considered using a combination of pilot red flesh meat and whiting worked best. They also used whiting and ling together.

19. In case your customers were hoping to hook a white you had to find pilot whales.

20. They seem to be in agreement that out-hooking a fish was better than jaw-hooking. Jaw fishing allowed the fish to play longer. Out fishing lessened the fish's fighting power since his innards took on the battle and it helped shorten the fight.

21. There was no time wasted on the return trip to port; mates examined and checked tomorrow's fighting equipment and rigs were set up for the next battle.

22. Rough water days can pose a problem to live rigs. Hooking up live bait the usual way behind the dorsal fin will be less productive since the bait eventually will be tossed sideways on the hook. Just hook the live bait through the upper jaw which will allow water to pass through the gills and breathing will be normal.

23. Finally, they all agreed that the use of nose to draw fish to a chum line, when nothing seemed to be hap-

pening and before moving to a new location, could bring surprising results. Nose attracted all types of game, big and small, by throwing an ashcan or cherry bomb as a depth-charger. It could perk the interest of the fish in the chum line.

24. Keep spare engine and boat parts on board; water pump, spark plugs, sand wires, starter motor, gas-air-oil filters, bulbs and fuses, windshield and motor wipers, etc. Be advised that there are no floating service stations at the continental shelf some seventy five miles off Montauk Point.

25. A number of Skippers had recorded in their logs an old phenomenon; upon returning to the docks with their fish, the gawkers would gather like a herd of dust stomping elephants. They were armed to the tusks with crowbars, teeth pullers, scalpels, bowie-butcher-carving knifes, screwdrivers, axes of all types, cleavers, hacksaws, chain saws, razors, claw hammers and, not to be outdone, a few supported machetes. Once your fish lay on the dock, the gawkers will surround it like flies on horse shit. Have the mates and customers stand guard over the fish. If need be, the Captain may have to pop a few shot gun blasts in the air, to warn the vultures. These scavengers are out for souvenirs and your fish is their keepsake. In a blink, teeth, jaw plates, fins, tail, etc. will disappear. One Skipper, recalled to

his horror, spotting his fish, sticking out of a car's trunk, tail flapping briskly, as the car moved down the road.

26. Their favorite fishing areas are: Jennie's Horn, Ryan's Horn, Fingers, The Owl, The Banana, Tyler's Gap, Atlantis, East and West Atlantis, Lobster claw, Big Eye Mountain, Hudson Canyon, Little fish Tail, FM Bank, Outter Butterfish, North-East-West Flats, The Claw, Gordon's Gully, Cox Ledge, Inside fingers and The Star. All were listed with accompanying waypoints.

Chapter 5

Calvin had an acquaintance who was a dealer in illicit goods. He was one Danny O'Malley who pretended to be a foulmouthed, calumnious man. Be that as it may, Calvin was not taken in by that act. Cal trusted Danny. They had a history of previous shady deals which included the use of Calvin's boat. Calvin never questioned Danny and Danny never offered. Danny had a passion for fulfilling customer's needs; no questions, just a nod of the head and a slight closing of the eyes. In this business it was essential to keep up both one's reputation and word. Shit, after all is said and done that's all one had in his line of work. A broken promise could shipwreck a fellow. However, Danny only filled the orders he knew were within the bounds of possibilities. You never argued with Danny; just paid his price and took your goods and left.

Danny was about 5' 11", had a stout build that supported a beer belly, curly dark brown hair that needed a washing and a four day old growth that was ever present. He was elusive in his manner, with shifty eyes that portrayed the cunning of a serpent. His appearance was slovenly but he spoke with an air of authority. Danny, no fool, knew always what was at stake and that it was his ass on the line; no slammer for him.

Salador's was Danny's hangout. He enjoyed the pool table and his Wild Turkey. Now, everybody liked Danny for his fair sportsmanship at both pool and cards. For fifteen years he had worked a tour on the draggers and longliners. That grind threw his body out of gear; he was "done in" as they say. He would often reflect on those trips and thought of the Captain up in that warm helm with his hot cup of coffee and whiskey while he occupied the cockpit that slowly crippled his body. "What a life," he laughed. His memory of that cold morning, long ago, when he woke up in his bunk paralyzed; hogtied, wasn't pleasant. The Coast Guard took him to Southampton Hospital where he later recouped. He knew then it was time to move on. At thirty five it was time to get into something new. He chose the dark side. "What the fuck, the money was great with minimum risks," he told himself. Ten years later he was driving a Mercedes Benz and residing in the Montauk Mews in a three bedroom condo with his live in girlfriend who was a tasty cook. He would come and go as he pleased; she never asked questions. Her life was very comfortable. "What more could one ask for?" she giggled. "What the hell, we all need some-one, right?" he thought.

Calvin met Danny that night; shook hands and played some poker. Danny knew instinctively that Cal was up to something, most likely to do with fish-ing. Calvin was always thinking about of those elu-sive fish. Danny knew his customers and that was a major fact for his survival. He was keenly sensitive to their needs, always reassuring them he would come through. Danny had needs, too. "You want, I get," was his philosophy. No matter what it took, Danny had crews out there to do most anything, provided that the pay was good and Danny paid well for their services. This arrangement kept them tight. Without them, his operation could wind up on a dragger. "No way," Danny maintained, "I'm up in the helm, no way back down to that loathsome, revolting, grotesque cockpit for me!" Danny spat.

Calvin knew the routine. Danny threw down a full house. Cal turned over four aces. Calvin thought Danny fucked up on the deal. He was supposed to get the full house. "Oh well, that's Danny," thought Cal. Danny smiled and Cal passed the envelope under the table. Excusing himself, Danny left for the men's room and read the envelope's contents. As he returned, he winked at Cal and put four hearts down on the table which signaled the delivery would be in four days. Cal shoved the pile of down payment money over to his buddy. Danny ordered another round of Wild Turkey while Calvin reassured himself that he had made the right move. The tournament was his! This was the final "sub rosa".

Danny O'Malley phoned Calvin at midnight three days later and said hurriedly, "Your place at 4:00am," and clicked off. Calvin hung up, turned around and strode over to the helm ladder, ascending into the cabin. He couldn't shake off that anxious feeling welling up in him. "Oh hell", he considered, "it must be all this planning and preparation for the upcoming shark tournament." He sat down in his Captain's chair, rested his head on the back, closed his eyes and let his hands fall in his lap. He had almost forgotten how comfortable this chair was. In fact, it was downright refreshing up here; so quiet and safe. "I'll have to come up here more often. No wonder Cary never emerges from these surroundings and comes down to the fighting deck unless she has to answer to the call of that stern voice of duty," Calvin reflected. "Cary's the best mate a Captain could have. She's responsible, reliable and most reasonable. She's keeping that cottage at Culloden Point hush-hush from me but in this village there are no secrets. It baffles human understanding how this shit gets out. Just go get a cup of coffee at Jack's place and you'll get enough buzz for a week. That's Montauk - any scandalous morsel is a choice bit of dirt." Cal vowed to himself, "When I win that damn tournament I'll pay off her remaining mortgage payments!"

Opening his eye and studying the bright stars, Calvin wondered how seafarers crossed the vast oceans by use of the stars, charts, compasses to navigate. Hell, they were real warriors of the high seas. Turning his attention back to Danny O"Malley, Calvin, talking aloud said, "Shit, he's a real paradox. He's between the devil and a peck of his troubles and a real good friend. His cleverness has put him in a sorry plight, and, one day, if worse comes to worse, it's all going to come crashing down, but, as they say, "c'est la vie".

Indeed, Danny was a man of few words. In his chosen profession brevity was essential to survival. Calvin wondered why Danny wound up in this line of work. It must have been the harsh labor on the draggers that broke his spirit. "I guess we all have our breaking point," Cal speculated, "but I don't have any plans on letting anything drive me off the deep end. What the hell possesses a person to sell their soul and wind up being chums with the devil? Such a repugnant alliance; that fulfilling mortal thirst of greed, money and power," he philosophized. "Hell, that's sure not me," he boasted. Further more, he deducted, one must be born, in a manner of speaking, with evil intent. Perhaps it was just waiting to blossom. Finally, one snaps and there's an evil coupling of his soul.

Calvin heard the truck pull up. "It's time," he reckoned, sensitive to the situation that was about to unfold as he recalled part of an old Scottish proverb; "the stilly hour when storms are brewing". Cal lifted himself out of the chair and climbed calmly down to the cockpit. Danny and his crew arrived on time. The men placed the fifty five gallon drums into the cockpit and left as suddenly as they had appeared. Danny shook hands with Cal, took his final payment and said, "It's fresh, just as you ordered, and, per your instructions, we added five gallons of hog blood to each drum. Shit, what in hell are you going for - Big White - JAWS?" Cal smiled and replied, "No, just some small mackerel," with a wink of his eye. Both had a good laugh. It also helped to relieve the tension on this cool, foggy night. Their hands released, Danny gave Calvin's shoulder a quick pat. "Later, big guy, keep in touch."

Cal stood there, eyeballing the stash, as if to ask him self a question, "How the hell can I lose the tournament with this shit? "To hell with the IGFA (International Game Fishing Authority) rules!" Mammal or flesh is strictly prohibited, Cal knew, but he also knew that he was a gamekeeper and this was war. "Now for the next phase," he chuckled.

Chapter 6

All boats required hours of maintenance while dockside. These duties were shared between the Captain and mate. One of Cary's responsibilities was to keep an eye on the freezer compartment to insure it was fully operational. She also made damn sure all spare parts were in good working order. Calvin was adamant about the freezer functioning to its optimum. Before leaving port to go out hunting he would inquire of Cary how the cold storage was doing. She would give him the affirmative nod and say, "Cap, everything is functioning properly, temperature just right and holding; spare parts are in sound working order." That's all Calvin needed to hear. He never doubted her word and would shoot back, "Great, Cary, keep a sharp eye on her. She's our life line. Without her we would be in one hell of a predicament."

Cary reassured herself that no 'perfect storm' would be a scenario for them. That movie always haunted her thoughts. Aboard the "Andrea Gail" their freezer, loaded with tuna, broke down and they were shit out of spare parts. Based on the freezer malfunction and big tuna money they made a decision to buck the storm and cash in. They could have chosen to dump the fish and stay safe, out beyond the reach of the storm, but they all voted to go for it. That decision eventually put both the tuna and them at the bottom of the sea. "Hell," Cary further thought, "I don't want my name ending up on the missing at sea plaque. Out on the open water you have to be prepared for any eventuality and as Calvin insists, always be prepared."

Calvin returned from the Yacht Club, jumped on board and found Cary up in the helm bent over toying with fuse box. "How are the fuses holding up, Cary?" he asked. She smiled one of her reassuring smiles, "They're okay, Skipper, no corrosion on the contacts but I cleaned them just to make sure we have plenty of spare ones as backup for all of them." Calvin said quietly, "We have to talk."

Taking on a more formal attitude, he eased himself into the Skipper's chair slowly. Cary followed the lead and sat down in her mate's seat, leaned forward and looked directly at Calvin. She knew this side of

Calvin and she paid full attention to his every word. Calvin began by telling Cary that he had been to the Island Yacht Club that morning and placed his wager of fifteen thousand down on the first place heaviest mako category. "We were issued tournament number thirteen and it has to be prominently displayed on the port side of the cabin window," and handed her the ten by ten inch entry card. Cary took it apprehensively. Calvin noting her look of disgust, asked, "What, Cary, what?" Cary rolled her eyes and could barely let out the words, "We're number THIRTEEN!" Calvin couldn't help it and went into a fit of laughter, pounding his thighs. He could hardly catch his breath and gasped, "Shit, not you, Cary. I don't believe it, not after what we've been through! I can't fathom that you believe in those old wives tales." Cary attempted to get rid of the card but Calvin put up his hand to fend it off. With that, Cary, snapped back sharply, "Get another number, any number, but thirteen!" Calvin jumped up from his chair, broke into laughter once again and roared out, "Hell, mate O'Shea, I presume you also believe in black cats, dream catchers and broken mirrors, too?" Cary swallowed down hard and yelled back, "Stop laughing, this is a serious superstition in part of my heritage. My mother taught us to knock on wood and keep our fingers crossed when we saw a black cat. So, stop laughing, Cal," as her blood pressure rose and her face became flushed.

Calvin saw her disconcerted glare and understood this was no laughing matter. As they say, 'if looks could kill', Miss O'Shea was in a very hostile mood. In fact, she was burning mad. Damn, Calvin thought, this is going to cost me 'a pound of flesh'. She's becoming a sea wolf. Shit, I never saw this side of her. Oh well, let's try another tact. "Cary," Calvin said quietly, "I didn't know you were so superstitious. You never mentioned it before this." Cary, replied, "No reason to," sitting there steaming with her arms folded.

Calvin also realized he was up against a hard stone; no use fighting this testy Cary. Though he never saw this side of her character before, oddly enough, he liked it. He thought it was almost like battling a monster fish. There was all this wonderful give and take until one succumbed finally to the struggle. Calvin knew he had to act quickly to regain his control of his feisty mate. He said softly, "Okay, okay, I'll take it back and get another number." Waiting for her to respond was an eternity. "Shit," Cal thought, "I never had a problem with Cary 'til this silly number thirteen came into play. She's always obeyed my orders, now she's giving orders. Shit, what the hell has happened to my Skipper Hood?"

At last Cary spoke, "Get another number or get another mate." Calvin was thunderstruck. "What the hell did you say?" "You heard right, Cal, new number or new mate." Those words cut into his innermost heart's core and its pain touched his very soul. Its hardness settled deep within him. He had never dealt with such a feeling in his life. "Okay, I'll get a new number, shit, I'll get all the fucking numbers you want, but, don't ever and I mean ever threaten me with 'new mate.'" He roared, "Do you understand me, Miss O'Shea?" pounding his two fists down hard on the Captain's chart table causing everything to explode and scatter to the floor. "Shit, he's pissed," thought Cary. Ranting on, he said, "We've been together for eleven years and I've always taken good care of you. Don't you dare say these words to me ever again. I'm your Captain, remember that woman, through thick and thin. Don't you ever threaten me; ever." Calvin slammed the table once more. Red faced and trembling, he turned and walked out down to the cockpit. He hopped on the dock and walked hastily away before Cary's tearful face could stop him. "I did it this time," she uttered. "Why couldn't I keep my mouth shut? To hell with my Mom's stupid superstitions, I'm losing my man."

Calvin was furious, really pissed off big time. He was cut to the heart by her words. Leave me, shit, no way, Miss O"Shea. I won't allow that, no fucking way! We're a team damn it and I'll do what I have to do to keep you, lady. Calvin guessed there was more to this than he had suspected. His emotions were running high; was he finally harboring a feeling of fondness toward her? Or was there something else since they had worked together these past eleven years. Have I been falling in love with her? I won't lose her; she's part of the boat and part of me. We're one on the ocean; a breed long gone. Calvin tried to console himself as he said aloud, "Hell, she's the mirror of my heart, my soul. No way, Miss O'Shea, am I going to lose you! I'll get a new number but let's hold no 'sharp tooth unkindness' between us, Miss Cary O'Shea. Perhaps, we should tie the knot after the tournament. How's about that, Mrs. O'Shea Cain? That might be the right course for us. Why not? We've been together for all these years and your little white cottage in Culloden with that fireplace might be just a good final resting place."

Calvin return to the Island Yacht Club and appealed his case to Captain Harding, Chairman of the tournament. The Captain acknowledged his sensitivity to the dilemma but stated adamantly the rules strictly prohibited changing a boat's number. And, further, numbers could not be interchanged since the boat name was printed on the number card. These rules were established so all contestants would have a fair shake, he added. Calvin was already in a foul mood and this explanation increased his anxiety. He rose his voice two timbres and said, "The hell you tell me, screw the rules. I demand a different number," as he moved closer to Harding.

Captain Folger, Senior Chairman, observing the situation getting rapidly out of hand, intervened and offered, "Captain Cain, sir, if you will, I have a suggestion that may meet with your approval." Calvin turned his attention to Folger, "Okay, what?" Captain Folger, explained, "Your boat shall go to the last position, as they say, 'bring up the pack' and you can change your number to one thirty three. Your mate is just a woman; she'll never know the difference, Cap." Calvin was just about to punch Folger out but held back his rage, thinking, okay, if this works, Cary's good nature would return. Calvin moved chest to chest to Captain Folger and looking down at him, spoke in a low tone, "Okay Cap, we'll 'bring up the pack' but know this, Captain Folger, sir, Cary is not just a woman. She's my mate and a damn good one at that; good enough to become my future wife." That said, Calvin swung around and walked through the doorway and back to his truck. He threw the new number card in the back and drove away.

Cary was up in the helm. Calvin shouted out, "Cary, we're the last of the pack; number one thirty three. Does that do it for you?" Cary opened the cabin door, looked down at Cal, and replied in a loving

voice, "Thank you, Skipper, I knew you could do it."
"Go home now, Cary, and get a good night's rest. I
need you, mate, and I'm grateful for you. You are my
little fishing friend and I never want to lose you." Cary
murmured to herself, "I'm in love at long last. I got to
him! Let's take it a little at a time, like Mom said, 'just
dangle some fresh bait.'"

Chapter 7

With Cary packed off, Calvin up in the helm, swung the boat out of her berth and maneuvered her to the marina pumping station. The gas attendant secured the vessel and asked, "How many gallons, sir?" Calvin blinked and his head recoiled when his eye glimpsed the price per gallon; $4.99. He yelled down in staggering disbelief to the attendant, "Are you kidding me? Five dollars a gallon for diesel fuel, how the hell did it go up two dollars within two weeks?" Calvin got even hotter under his collar and continued sputtering to himself, "Shit, even the twenty five pound cans of chum have tripled in price. It's a hellish seventy five dollars a can now. Talk about extortion, this is downright robbery."

The attendant watched and listened, shaking his head, as the red faced Calvin, spewed on, "Now it's against the law to buy bait from the draggers due to environmental wackos and their endangered species list. How the hell are we to make a living at these prices? They're shaking us down and sooner or later I'll be walking around 'naked as a needle.'"

The attendant, standing there, tapping his foot, shouted up to Calvin, "Sir, the owner is in his office watching a DVD, why don't you go ask him? I get paid only $6.50 to pump this shit. Every Skipper that pulls in here gives me the same crap and I'm not getting paid enough to take this aggravation. So, what'll be, sir, fill her up or untie her?" Calvin caught himself, no sense taking it out on this poor lad; it's the fault of the government over taxation and surcharges up the ass. In a kinder tone, Calvin said, "Okay, you're right, it's not your fault, you're underpaid, so, lad, fill her up."

As soon as Calvin maneuvered his boat out of the inlet, he observed that the water was like a mirror, smooth and even. Cal gave it full throttle and "Shark Killer II" responded accordingly. Her engine purred with a high pitch sound as she cut the water like a great orca with an ever so slight roll to compensate for the water drag on her bow. At full speed, in flat water, she was mindful of her lord and master at the helm. Cal felt her power thrust them both forward, finally trimming off. "Hell," Cal exclaimed, "tis a thing of beauty only a Captain and boat could share."

As Calvin rounded the lighthouse, he set course southeast toward the Horn's fishing grounds. The trip would be another hour and a half. He figured the sun would be setting just as he had planned. As they say, "out of sight, out of mind". He did not want to call attention to his next move. Calvin was deploying all matters of deception that one could possibly do out on open water.

Upon his arrival at the Horn, he powered down to his waypoint mark in the stillness of the cool evening breeze. He used his glasses to scan 360 degrees; no sight of boat activity. "Good," he smiled, "I'm alone." He had chosen this particular area because it had proven to be very productive for him and Cary. But even better, his two dragger Captain friends had been sending him hot information. They reported seeing a load of bait in this vicinity and spotted large makos and a few swordfish basking on top in the sun for the past two weeks. They also informed him that the other battle-grounds they had been dragging were cool; not much to report. Calvin paid them regularly for their intelligence gathering by buying them Wild Turkey and dinners at Salador's upon their return to port.

It was time to lower the O'Malley drums. Cal had prepared them with pre-measured line and anchors. The moon, in her full radiance, flirting in and out of the clouds, gave Cal the camouflage and light in which to work. Everything was cooperating, thought Cal; a good omen. He lowered the first drum off the stern. Satisfied, he continued, but, waited each time, until the boat drifted five feet to port, before lowering another drum, to insure proper spacing. He repeated this process four more times before all were anchored down fifteen feet below the sea surface and out of sight. Before launching a drum, he pushed the red button to start the timer. As pre-set, each drum liquid would open to release, a little at a time, the red-gold liquid. The current would take over and pick up bits, sailing them on an easterly course.

The timers were set to start to release at approximately 6:00am. Upon their arrival at 8:00am the next morning, if all went according to plan, the slick line should be well formed and defined. This chum would be attracting the big meat before they even arrived. Cal thought, that to their advantage, they would be hours ahead of the other boats. If things worked out, they would have their beast early and return to port shortly after mid day.

Calvin felt like an architect, a dreamer of things to come. He had complete faith in his make shift drum chum scheme. "Why, shit, it's the first of its kind in the world, and, better yet it's reusable," he marveled. "What the hell would Mundus think? He probably would be the only old salty dog to see its worth! I'll have to take a trip to Hawaii and shoot the shit with him. What a laugh that would be!"

Calvin made one last inspection of his drum line, started the engine and went full throttle back to port. Fully confident, he stood at the helm like a monolith, in all its grandeur. His spirits were high, swimming in expectations of what tomorrow should bring!

Chapter 8

The starter boat was one hundred yards outside the inlet. All tournament boats were lined up, one behind the other; engines roaring, anglers at the ready. The weather was perfect; five to ten mile an hour winds, sun up; warming the critters of the deep.

Cary sat in her mate's chair, Cal in the Cap's chair. Cary asked gingerly, "Cal, do you mind being last?" Cal turned his black bearded face, grinning cheek to cheek, and said mysteriously, as if he was harboring a dark secret, "The winds of change are ours. The truth is Cary, it doesn't matter what our number is. The stage is set and our chum line will soon be setting up. That puts us ahead of them!" Cary, jerked her head back, her face displayed full wonderment. "How's that possible, Cal, we're sitting at port?" she asked. Cal noticed the flare in the sky and watched it as it arched slowly back down to earth. "Trust me, Cary," he answered, "be patient and trust in your, Cap," as he moved the throttle ahead to keep up with the other boats.

As they rounded the inlet, Calvin gave it full throttle and said to Cary, "Keep her sharp on course. I'm going below to set up the equipment and check the freezer. Call me as soon as we get to the Light and that's an order!" He left Cary to her thoughts. Her thinking was all a buzz. What's he up to? Chum lines set up, how's that possible? Wait a minute, where are those drums we had on board yesterday? What about the air about him today, like he's playing with a full deck of marked cards? He's hoodwinking me. I know he's up to something but that something will just have to wait. Okay, Skipper, I'll be patient and wait. Shit, there's nothing else I can do. She pushed the throttle up as far as it would go. The "Shark Killer, II" was back on the hunt.

As per instructions, Cary shouted out the window, "Cal, we're at the Light." He entered the helm and studied the traffic. As he suspected, they were all heading on courses north and easterly; no one was heading southeast. Cal set his waypoint on his GPS and noted time of arrival one and a half hours. "Cary, let me know when we're five miles from arrival." "Aye,

Aye, Cap," she saluted. Cal went below to finish setting up and take a snooze.

Cary turned on the intercom and gently eased Cal out of his dream world. "Cal, we're five miles out." Cal returned to the helm, holding two cups of mud; gave Cary hers and asked, "Do you see it Cary?" "I don't see shit but those birds circling above the water means there must be some kind of bait over there." Cal announced proudly, "Cary, that's our chum line already forming and by my judgment of the currents and the wind it's most likely a half mile long and fifteen feet wide. And my best guess is that critters are already on the scent!" Cary turning to Cal smiling, and laughing said, "I don't know how the hell you did this, Cal, but you have outdone yourself this time. Holy shit, a well formed chum line at arrival! That's just out of this world! How the hell did you pull this off?" Cal said simply, toying with her, "Cary, that's why I am Cap!" She shook her head and sipped her mud. They were both in high spirits and laughed all the way to the way-point marking; 40 45 800 71 27 000. Cal dropped his flag buoy. The business of monster fighting took on a new meaning.

Calvin could tell by the way the rod was reacting that it was a small mako, probably in the three hundred pound class. This was not the ticket. He released the fish to the depths but was encouraged. Cary gave him two thumbs up and prayed. She thought; this is what Cal lives for; he is at war. He takes the attitude that everything is in conflict with him. He's a quick tempered, cantankerous old salt. Guess that's what keeps his adrenaline flowing. Jesus, can't he ease up a little? God willing; wind and weather permitting and with some luck, he'll get his big meat. Hell, after all his preparations and those drums, how could he miss? Cary turned her head forward and scanned the horizon for a few moments. She evaluated their drift and slick speed; all was going well. She lowered her head a notch and renewed her praying, whispering, "Our Father who art in heaven....." in a humble and earnest way.

Calvin was throwing out all stops; he was going for the big one! That was his bet; fifteen thousand down on the heaviest shark division. No room for failure, this was all or nothing; catch or be damned. One thousand pounds would do just fine, he thought. Stop tormenting yourself and quit tempting the gods. I'll settle for a six or seven hundred pounder. Now I know it's up to the spirit of the sea. Come across, Neptune, you owe me one. In a loud voice aimed at the sea he said, "I've prepared myself for this bloody event and I don't want to run up against any foul ups now. I put my faith into the laps of the gods, unlike those other dream catchers in their fancy boats." He stood there like a Herculean statue; a tower of statue of strength, rocking port to starboard as the boat swayed in her sleepy drift.

Chapter 9

The slick was inviting and holding together unusually well. "Where are you big guy?" he yelled. Calvin reassured himself that somewhere close, down in those vast depths of blue waters, was his fish. He remembered that Mundus stretched the line as a non conformer. His approach was unorthodox. Throughout his fishing career, Mundus maintained his free spirit and easy style. Frank Mundus was a showman; he was wonderously strange. Cal knew that Mundus, an exceptional Captain, howled with the wolves. He was a stand alone maverick, toying with the new fish catching contraptions and developing a practical, hard earned knowledge of shark behavior. Calvin reasoned that Frank was a man of ideas; he never joined the chorus. He was known to utter those yeahs, uh huh and um um hums. Damn, Calvin thought, he would sure in hell love to get Frank's take on his new submerged floatation drum apparatus that automatically creates a chum slick. "Why, hell, it's a labor saving device! In addition, there's a new pump system on the drums in the stern of my boat. It's my fluid drive chumming system!" Cal relaxed and grinned inwardly with a sense of satisfaction knowing that Frank would most likely say, "um hums" that being his nod of approval. Personally, that would mean a great deal to Calvin; another maverick in his own time. Cal reflected wistfully that Mundus could smell them there critters. "I wish I had his nose," Calvin sighed.

Cal sensed his fish was swimming somewhere out there like a destroyer seeking the next meal. He envisioned the hook up; not too quick, you know the rules. Give him room and let that sharp curved hook set itself. Be patient. Once you snag that mighty, all devouring, elusive creature the melee begins! Remember, at first do a strong, long pull backwards, bringing the rod tip up hard and lay your shoulders back 'til they catch fire. Fight off the tension fatigue. This encounter is between you and him. It comes simply down to who wears out whom. Once he's hanging from the gin pole there will be enough time to lick your wounds.

Standing at his battle station, his mind razor sharp and that dark eye forever searching the wet, cool, blue water, he was in the stream of consciousness of all around him. It was harsh reality like the kind that parts the boys from the men. Calvin was born to fish and he knew he was one of the best. Surely he thought, God gave him his massive bulk for just that purpose.

Cal could hold his own when battling huge monsters. When he was just beginning his fishing career he worked as a mate on various charter boats. He learned hard and fast how to play a fish, when to give and when to take. He was a superior fish handler; once they were hooked, as they say, "you were dead meat". Given that aside, what really impressed the Skippers of the charter boats was his fighting tenacity; his staying power. Shit, he never gave up the pole. He would stand there and fight, never handing off the rod. Occasionally, until the skippers got to know Cal better, they offered to take the rod and give him a rest. Cal just looked at them in their eyes, smiled back and shook his head back and forth and continued the fight. There were battles that lasted four hours. Never did he show signs of fatigue. The Captains and crew watched, shaking their heads in awe. Shit, this guy was good!

Maintaining his guard and vigilantly keeping his nose to the wind and his weathered eye to the sky, Calvin continued to think positively. Yet, it pained him to know he had lost his eye and he recalled that old Scottish saying, "the precious treasure of his eyesight lost" from a children's pirate book. As he watched the horde of terns and seagulls circling above the chum line he observed their more frequent dives to steal his precious bait. "Shit, enough is enough," he shouted, "I paid hard earned money for that chum." He turned around and was about to yell at Cary, "Get the twelve-gauge!" Shit, is she good or is she good? Cary, as though reading his mind, was at the ready, holding the shot gun and awaiting orders. Cal said laughingly, "Cary, rid me of those damn looting flying feathered beggars." No sooner had he uttered those words, Cary slipped off the safety and pumped the trigger four times. When the smoke cleared, the moochers were high tailing it south! A few leftovers became bait themselves as they fell out of the warm sky into the chum line. Calvin remarked approvingly, "Good shooting, Cary. That got rid of those predators."

Just as they were about to have another good laugh, Calvin saw Cary point east at ten o'clock. His eye caught sight of the tell tail trademark of a blue shark with that floppy upper lobe on his tail. Sure in hell he was on the scent of the chum. Every once in awhile his head would burst out of the water, thrashing back and forth, as his jaw tore apart another slab of bait. Cary shouted down, "He's twenty yards from your free swimming blue fish; for sure he's going to grab it. Cal, he's under, get ready!" Calvin did not have to coax the blue shark on. He was after the scent and going for it. Calvin knew Mr. Shark would strike hard and fast, particularly since he was a hungry critter. Blues prefer live bait to dead chum. Calvin also knew what was coming and felt the vicious hit. He threw his reel into gear and set that rusty old looking hook right into the critter's jaw. Catching sharks, in general, is like playing a chess game; the shark makes the opening move. Grab the bait and run! Calvin felt his weight; nice; close to one hundred and fifty pounds. He'll make a nice snack for big boy.

Blue sharks make their first run the longest and hardest. On average they can run 150 to 200 yards, more or less, depending on their size. Calvin had hooked this one but good; he used a martu hook. He employed its use because it had a sharp point and sturdy barb which made for a solid setting in the shark's jaw. In the middle game, Calvin used to what he referred to as shark logic. The shark was testing Calvin's fishing ability. Is he a novice or does he know his shit? Calvin allowed him to make his futile moves and then began to hammer him home, hauling him back on the rod tip, bringing the critter even close to the vessel. Here played out the life and death struggle.

Chapter 10

Approaching the middle game was pure pulse hopping excitement; the critter's unpredictability came into play. One never knew what turn of events the battle would take. The critter's battle tactics could develop a new twist and all shit could break loose. The fish would try to play the odds in his favor and the angler depended on his aptness to outfox the beast. One had to have all one's wits in alert working order when fighting the creature. The struggling critter on the other end of the line took on an additional uglier attitude. Talk about mean spirited, he was down right blood thirsty; a cold hearted, cold blooded beast; son of a bitch! The critter had an evil inbred into him through generations of sharks. The closer you wrenched him boat side, the more vicious his temper became. His resentment to being hooked was played out by his spinning and thrashing.

As one entered into the end of the game one had to remain sharp. This was a dark eyed monster and his existence had a two fold purpose: to hunt and spawn other sharks. Thus, he fought savagely to survive another day at sea. Calvin sensed the struggle ending. He labored hard hauling the critter even closer to the boat. Cary was at the ready with a flying gaff. Calvin brought the beast alongside and Cary gaffed him. She handed Cal the 30/30 rifle and took his rod. Calvin pumped two shots behind his head and all went silent. The critter's fight for survival was over.

Captain and mate tail-tied him and winched him on board. Cary watched safely from up in the helm as Cal cut the critter down the middle; his innards fell on the floor. Assuming that Calvin was going for the liver since it's good eating fried up, Cary was surprised he decided to use it for bait. Yet she knew its scent was like a love potion for the big guys. They could not resist its sweet oily fragrance. Calvin put the liver in the chum box and lowered it into the water, securing the box to the stern cleat. Winking at Cary, he proceeded to cut a slab in a rectangular shape, approximately fourteen inches long by five inches wide and four inches thick, removed the dark skin from the back side and saved the firm, bright white meat for them. He then hooked his prize on his deep rig pole and held it up for Cary's approval. Smiling and waving, she caught his second wink, as he heaved the critter's remains out of sight into the deep blue water.

In the suspense of marking time and waiting for signs of big fish activity, Calvin fell into a twilight of sleep; not unusual, for most old salts could sleep while standing on their feet. Calvin thought; no fighting chair for me. That's what those city imbeciles, who would rather sun bathe or catch up on their sleep at six hundred dollars a trip, would do. His rod set securely in his gimbal belt while he waited. Day dreaming brought him back to the time his father had taken him big mouth bass fishing in Montauk Lake at ten years of age. But, suddenly, Cary yelled with breathless impatience, "Calvin, large gray dorsal fin, starboard, two o'clock; half mile out! Big meat just entered the slick and appears to be damn interested, damn interested!" Disregarding her shouting he drifted back to that wonderful cherished, sun lit day, pressed in his memory, when his father shouted with the same excited zeal, "Calvin, your bobber just shot down!" Sleep had encased his small frame, his eyes grew heavy as his head tilted to his left shoulder and was bobbing up and down. His father, totally engulfed in a state of panic, stumbled as he tried to reach Cal. He shouted once again with added authority "Calvin, pull your rod tip back, straight back!" In a half stupor, Calvin obeyed robotically and pulled his rod tip back with all the strength his little muscles could muster. BAM, he had his first hook up and his adrenalin shot into his blood stream; heart thumping and pulse pounding. The excitement overwhelmed the young lad. Yet, like all young boys do, when their dad's yell at the top of their lungs, he followed his dad's instructions. As the fish neared the shore line, the water was shallow and the fish knew by instinct that this was his final chance for freedom. The bass went into his death dance; a battle strategy of thrashing and spinning about in anticipation of spitting out that unholy hook. Calvin anticipated the bass' moves and by this time was alert and ready. At the right moment, he surged forward and captured the bass in the net. The fish became subdued; its eyes seemed to be studying the pattern of the mesh net. Dad held him high and turned to Calvin with a triumphant glow of pride. He ran splashing through the water, reached Calvin and said, "Son, you did it," smiling broadly, cheek to cheek and patted Cal on the shoulder like men do only when they have bonded by a marvelous event.

Calvin was the talk of the hamlet for a whole week. He had hooked a sixteen pound big mouth bass, thus, setting the record in Montauk! Half the town grabbed their poles and headed to the Lake, having great expectations of their own prize bass. You know - the pot of gold at the end of your hook! As the week wore on the

frantic fishing eased up, rods found their sleepy nooks,
once again, in the dark closets.

Chapter 11

Cary shouted again from the helm, "Cal, Cal, he's on his way to your blue shark bait!" Once more, she yelled, at the top of her lungs, to be heard over the roar of the diesel engine, "He's fifty yards from your bait and tracking; zeroing in!" His fin size gave every indication that the monster was in the five to six hundred pound class. Cary yelled again, "He's on the scent of your bait and heading straight for it. Get ready!"

Calvin perked up. He could sense her excitement. She was a good old gaffer and always there, eagerly edging him on. Taking a few breaths to clear his head he readied himself for this primitive, stealthy, gray torpedo. The more bulk, the bigger the bang, he figured. He recalled his father's cool analogy concerning his trophy fish; it's a love hate relationship. Love is holding the rod and reel. Hate is fighting for his life; doing everything to spit or shake free of that steel, rusty shank anchored into his jaw. Calvin opened his eye and saw the crook coming down his pike. This battle was not a game of who wins, it's a must win for me; Captain Calvin Cain.

The beast hit hard and fast, then shot forward, north at twelve o'clock at full throttle heading for the horizon and breached three times. At two hundred and fifty yards out he slowed down and stayed on the surface. Good, Cal knew, better that going deep. It's hell or nearly impossible for one man to bring up a beast of this size. Cal shouted to his fish, "Stay topside!" Cary heard Cal and yelled, "Stay topside!" Calvin knew this tug of war was an affair of honor, "fight the good fight beast but this conflict will end," Cal shouted, mockingly. "I'll be left and you, big fella, will be just another wondrous charm of a battle of man-eating memory!"

Calvin's bulk was one sorry, awful ache and pumping like a reactor. He fought the beast for nearly an hour while he put on a frenzied show, fighting ferociously and incorporating a number of beastly tactics, not fooling Calvin, however. Past encounters hardened him to these "shark" deceptions. "Do your best, Mr. Shark," Calvin taunted, "Make my day!" Cal's hands were welded to the reel's fighting handle and rod. His legs were working on all cylinders. They behaved like pistons, up and down, up and down, pulling, pumping and hammering the beast home.

His will and confidence grew stronger the closer the beast yielded to the boat. Sensing that the beast was fried, almost spent out, Cal shouted triumphantly, "Just a matter of yards, you know, big fella." Shortly, the beast capitulated to his unrelenting master. Calvin's elation started to cool down his machinery. "No time for celebration," he grinned, "next, have to get this critter on board; plenty of time for relaxation and merrymaking when my job is done."

This was no paper doll on the end of his line, Cal sure in hell knew. He also knew the beast was no quitter. When he realizes his predicament boat side, his evil nature will kick in. He'll do anything and everything to gain his freedom. Unpredictability determines the nature of his behavior, Cal thought, and as one man put it, "it's not over 'til it's over.'" "This nasty battle sure ain't over yet. I'll have to cool his heels," Cal planned, and shouted "hey, big fella, chill out! I have a chuck wagon of goodies to offer Your Lordship. My arsenal consists of rifles, shotguns, revolvers, battle axes, machetes, gaffs, spears, clubs and lastly - dynamite! What's your pleasure, big fella?" The beast answered with a counter offer; a ferocious crushing of his jaw down on the portside hull. He went into a pounding, mashing spiral dance; thrashing against the side of the boat. All six hundred plus pounds were attempting to pulverize the hull in expectation of sinking her; dinner time guys!

Little damage was done for his futile effort against the ten inch hard wood frame. The beast paid the price; a number of teeth were sunken awkwardly into the wood. After this romp, Calvin reconsidered jousting with the fish and willed himself to end the critter's torment. Don't get fooled by this big fella, he's still got fight in him yet, he thought. As if on cue, the beast quieted and succumbed to fatigue. Cary, watching the action, knew there was little time to do her job. Once the beast calms down there is little time to end his nomadic life. Sharks can regenerate at a surprising fast rate. Then all hell can break loose. Cary noted there was no sign now of spinning or rolling which is their natural habit along boat side. She hurried down to the cockpit and made ready.

Calvin held his pole at a forty five degree angle while Cary stood next to him, wearing her heavy duty gloves, in order to handle the wire leader. Together they moved like two ballerinas in slow motion. There was no talking, no orders, just teamwork. Cary handed Cal the thirty- thirty caliber rifle and very carefully took hold of the wire leader. Calvin secured the rod into his makeshift gimbal holder on the portside gunnel. Freed now from his rod, Calvin could grab the pole effortlessly and battle the beast, if he tried to make a run for it, back to portside. Calvin took aim to the back of his head, careful not to pop the wire leader, switched off the safety and discharged four shots, dispatching this beauty to shark paradise.

Through hard earned experience, the tricks of their trade kicked in. Both knew that this was no time to drop one's guard. Even in death the beast could be lethal even in his dying passing, that "dreamless sleep" he could lash out one more time with his steel jaw and sever one's arm or slice a person in two. Calvin secured the rifle's safety and placed it on the cockpit floor. He slid to Cary's left side, picked up the fifteen foot gaff, grasped the tail-tie rope and put its loop on the pole. He gaffed the tail, pulling it out of the water about two feet, slid the rope down the pole and eased it around the tail. Now that the tail was roped, he could hitch the other end of the rope to the automatic left ring. Both moved back to a safe distance, in case, while being lifted, the beast did a "C" or "U" turn move, followed by a crunching snap of its jaws one final time. It could simply be a muscle reflex; it's been known to happen. Hell, the critter doesn't know he's dead, Cal thought, as he slowly winched him up, stopping at the dorsal fin. The beast's head hung two feet above the water. Cary eyeballed him for the slightest movement. As she was about to approach him, Calvin raised his hand. Cary froze like a statue, while Calvin whammed the beast with the gaff pole several times, until satisfied of no movement. The fish, with its dull black eyes, hung there motionlessly. Once again Cary scanned the beast and approached gingerly, on the ready to escape, at the slightest twinge.

Her eyes burned from staring so long at that gigantic jaw; no teeth for me, she thought! Swinging a rope behind the dorsal fin and catching the end of the rope as it rounded the fish, Cary performed like an acrobat who caught swinging bars in mid air. She tied a hangman's knot and pulled the rope hard until the knot slid down and secured the middle of the beast. She handed Calvin the other end of the rope and went up to the helm. Safe at last! Calvin knew the capacity of weight his gin pole could hold; approximately two tons. The critter would do just fine after he secured the middle rope to another gin pole ring.

Calvin resumed winching until the beast was, as they say, "hanging high". Cary smiled, not too wide of a smile, just enough to show approval. She knew Cal was no boaster; just a humble fisherman with his prize on board. At the top of the gin pole Calvin attached four shower heads, in order to keep the beast wet.

Looking through an assortment of corks, he found the right ones he needed to plug up the four bullet holes that were oozing blood. "Have to prevent weight loss; every pound counts," he reiterated. Next he turned on the water which ran up the hose and out through the shower heads and wetted down the entire creature. "No loss through evaporation," he chuckled. The last chore involved the use of a large black canvas to surround the fish and keep the sunlight off its body. The tarpon reached to the top of the gin pole keeping the beast cool. Calvin grinned, "I'll bet Mundus would get a kick out of this!"

Chapter 12

The run back from Ryan's Horn took approximately two hours. Cary turned the boat's wheel hard to port and guided her smoothly into the inlet. People fishing off the jetties pointed, dropping their jaws, in twisted amazement, peering wide eyed in awe at the sight unfolding before them. In all his splendor there was the bewildering view of the beast hanging from the gin pole. Talk about making an entrance, this was "pride, pomp and circumstance," all wrapped in one princely debut, Cary mused. Above the beast, at the very top of the gin pole, was the shark flag, flying proudly; grandstanding to the galleries. The gawkers fumbled excitedly to ready their cameras into action.

Calvin put on his usual all star show for the tourists. It was good for the chartering business. It was also one of those unmentioned allures to snare new customers and to whet the appetite of the thrill seekers. While the appeal in Montauk was that the locals would ride around in their SUV'S displaying their rods, flashing in their rod holders, which were attached to the front fenders or poles in the roof racks, their purpose was to support the village tackle shops. As a fishing hamlet, Montaukers put out whatever bait necessary to keep the money flowing. Hence; the shark and tuna tournaments, etc.

Cary relaxed the throttle as they entered the marina. She turned the boat around skillfully and pulled up to the weigh station. The official announcer was informing the crowd of the Captain, mate and boat's name. He added a little fill to keep them from getting bored; describing the beast's features and guessed at the weight. "Folks, you may be looking at the big winner," he teased. Everybody cheered, pointed and drank their drinks, holding them high. As usual, there were the camera freaks photographing family members in line with the beast and the boat; another album filled.

Calvin winched his beast down, resting him on the cockpit floor and handed the tie-tail rope to the deck hand. He tied it to their land winch and his partner hoisted big fella up for the official weigh in. After all was said and done, big fella hit the scale, topping off, at six hundred and forty pounds. Calvin turned to Cary

and gave one of those elusive winks and a huge bearded smile. He won; she knew, proud to be his mate.
"End of mortgage payments," she sighed. "What a life,
thank you Lord." She strolled off the helm and shook
Calvin's hand. The two stood there and watched while
the cameras rolled and the flashes blinked.

At 4:30pm Cary and Calvin went to the bar for a
cold one. They moved through the crowd to the back
room reserved for crew members and ordered their
cold beers and two sandwiches. The various tournament crews stopped by to give their compliments and
all the other kind of bullshit. It was now 5:30pm, only
one half hour before six o'clock. Calvin urged the minute hand to a quick march, "Let's end this tournament,"
he almost said out loud. Abruptly, the speaker system
screeched. The announcer blared out the news of a
possible rival beast coming through the inlet.

Cary and Calvin's eyes locked frozen as they held
their beers up to their mouths. They both felt a numb-
ness tingling up their spines; breathing was forced. It
would be only a matter of minutes before the new possible trophy would make its appearance and hoisted
up for weigh in. They made their way out to the upper deck and watched as "Heavenly Father III" pulled
in reverse and came slowly in stern first. Cary prayed
as she tried to estimate the new beast's weight. Cal-

vin stared; he figured, "shit, it's going to be close;" all or nothing; that was his bet. "Lord, I'm not a praying man but please have mercy on me. Why, with all the planning and work, please let our big fella here hold the win," he prayed.

As they hoisted up the new beast, the scale tipped at six hundred, forty seven. The announcer yelled, "The new winner! Folks, we have a new winner!" Cary, holding back her tears, prayed, "Not here, not now, Lord, not among these people, especially Calvin." Later, back at her cottage, she knew, would be time to release those aching sobs and free herself of that tortured man's plight. Cary knew Calvin best. She knew he needed time to regroup. "I feel his hurt. Best to let him be. I'll wait for his call."

As Calvin watched the scale tip at 647 pounds he experienced the pain of "a bite from a thousand teeth". Within him arose a vexation of his spirit, blackened by a disquieted disgust; a haunting wretchedness engulfed his being. "So this is hell," he tormented, feeling he was going in to some kind of shock. He had to get a grip and quick; others were watching. He turned slowly and forced his legs to rise and then fall, finally taking the necessary steps that would get him back to his boat.

Calvin headed down the stairs to the lower cabin. It was dark and quiet. He tumbled to the floor on his knees, weakened by the events of the day. He grieved, "Seven pounds, just seven pounds, lost by seven pounds, now, I know what the word loser means. They won, I lost."

He laughed quietly, then louder until he felt an odd fear. Suddenly, like a thunder clap, he let out a long ghostly wail followed by tears that burned and rained hard and heavy, cascading down to the boat's floor. It was the "tempestuous rage" and it had Calvin by its jaws. When his tear duct had no more liquid to discharge his upheaval was over. Now he would have all the time he needed to contemplate "his sea of troubles".

He brooded on his boat for two weeks. To his dismay and embarrassment, he knew he was the buzz of the fleet. Cary stayed away. The time to comfort him or to inform him would come later. The other Captains respected his fish; job well done. But she knew there could be no talking to him while he was cut to the heart. "Let him agonize, he'll get over it and besides we got good money for the mako," Cary tried to reason. "Time will diminish that tortured soul. He usually finds a way to make the best of it when he gets the worst of it," she trusted.

Calvin's relief came as he rolled over his plans for his new project that he had been mulling over in his mind for the past two weeks. He called Cary and told her, "Tomorrow, 5:00am, be on time, bring the lunch." Cary knew his lunch likes. "Okay, he's back! Let's go for it, big guy," she laughed. The quiet excitement she detected in his voice would be hidden from others but not from her. She said to herself, "I know that eye and I also know what's behind that black patch. His mind works 24-7. That's why he's one of the best among the fleet. Who else would have thought of using a small piper aircraft to spot swordfish basking on the top of the water or tracking down tuna, marlin, dead whales and even sharks on the move calling in weigh points to Cal? Yeah, he's the thinker, that Calvin. What the hell has he hatched now, I want to know! He lost the tournament. He bet it all on the biggest fish category, $15,000 he laid down: WINNER TAKE ALL! He lost to Captain Mark on the forty foot boat, "Heavenly Father III." Mark took over $200,000 cash prize money for the biggest fish. Damn, "Heavenly Father III " out-fished "Shark Killer II". Maybe Cal should think about renaming his boat, like "Lord II" or "Lord of Lords" or "Heavens Glory", something that doesn't offend the sea gods. Fishing can be as elusive as a boat's name. I'm going to talk to Calvin about this right after lunch. Only hope those tuna sandwiches and pickles put a beam on that black bearded face or maybe I'll just keep my mouth shut. Sometimes that works best. Mama said it right, "You can't control an old salt, just tease him with fresh bait"!

That afternoon Cary ate alone up on the deck. Calvin ate alone in the cabin. That morning, Cary had noticed some kind of gleam in his eye but she wasn't sure of what it meant. They picked a four hundred pound thresher which is the best eating fish of the shark folks and as luck would have it a one hundred and fifty pound mako; a good day's work in all. "This blue water will ease his pain away," Cary hoped, "there's a flame burning in that man, he'll get over those groans." Calvin seemed to have nine lives; he lost one this time. She was well aware that he knew the ups and downs of fishing. He would enter through another gate; a fresh start, she felt. His nature was like a morning march which would prevent him from falling into that downward slope and instead reach for the crown. There was an enigma about Cal that puzzled Cary. Right now he was leaving her out in the cold. "Oh well," she said, "let's wait and see what's to come."

Chapter 13

Todd waved good bye to his family as usual and finished his house hold chores. It was still early, only 8:30am, time enough to shoot the shit with the guys down at Jack's. He climbed into his truck and turned on his VHF, thinking, perhaps, there might be some fish chatter. As he pulled onto Second House road, a voice came on his radio, "Yeah, yeah, I was at Ditch Plains early this morning and picked three keepers and a bunch of schoolies." Todd recognized Joe's lingo, then there was silence. Joe came back, "the keepers were between twelve and fifteen pounds and fat." Then silence. Todd understood why he could hear only one side of the conversation; the other guy was out of his listening range. Joe returned, "How did you do at Shagwong?" Again silence. Todd wished he could hear the reply. Joe returned, "Really, what time did they break?"

Todd turned onto Main Street, headed down town to Jack's and, finally within range, he heard Charlie say, "At first light 'til 7:30." Joe answered, "Fine, maybe I'll head that way after work. Talk to you later, Charlie, I've a job to do. You have my cell number; give me a call if there's any action." Todd grabbed his mike and said, "Hey, Joe, where are you?" "I'm heading home, have to get Dad's breakfast ready and go out on a job, a big job, setting up a new house with all the plumbing. Jake and I will be working this all week." "How about I treat you to a cup of coffee at Jack's? I want to talk to you about the new rod I'm building for you." "Thanks, Todd, but not today, my schedule is tight. Catch you in a couple of days. By the way I could use a few jars of Jamie's red-gold tomato sauce. Leave them in the garage in the freezer and take the blue plastic bag. There's three pounds of flounder there for you; had a good catch of those rascals yesterday. Say hello to Jamie for me and tell her that her sauce is great. Charlie had fish at the Wong this morning, a mixed bag of schoolies and keepers. Take care, Todd." Just like that Joe was gone; Todd hung up his mike.

As he pulled up to Jack's, Stuie was walking out. Todd called, "Hey, Stu, do you have any scallops?" Stu grinned and said, "Yeah, they're in the freezer. Your name is on the plastic container. Two quarts, right?" Todd shook his head, "Yeah, the wife and kids love 'em.

Damn sweet, Stu, the best tasting ever!" "Is that right, everybody's been telling me that same shit, even Mom said these are the best ever. You know, you have your good years and then those off years." Todd handed Stu the money as Stue said, "Pick them up whenever Mom's home. I've deliveries to make, catch you at the beach." Todd watched as Stu pulled away and said to himself, "The job of a bayman is never done. He's out on the water at sunrise hauling oysters, clams, scallops and fishing up a storm. Damn tough work. All I have to do is unlock the store, dust the bottles and taste the wines the dealers are trying to sell me. But I wouldn't trade places with Stu! Shit, shucking three hundred scallops each morning and that back breaking raking clams and oysters, no way, not for me!"

As Todd entered the coffee house, Jack started to pour his coffee and placed it on the counter. He knew Todd preferred the counter to the tables. Jack asked, "Just coffee, Todd, or can I make you up some ham and eggs, your favorite?" "Had breakfast, Jamie made Stuie's scallops and eggs. You should put them on your menu, Jack." "At $20 a pint? These boys can't afford that. Shit, they're bacon and eggs men. But these city folks think it's a Montauk delicacy and have no problem when I hand them the bill. Shit, Todd, could you imagine me handing Joe, the plumber, a bill for $35 for breakfast? Hell, he'd shut off my water." They both laughed at the thought of Jack handing Joe a $35 breakfast bill.

It was a mixed bag at Jack's; a few locals, mostly tourists. Most of the locals at this hour were at work or on the beach. Todd saw Mike, Tom and Eric sitting in the corner, huddled over their breakfast dishes and steaming third cups of coffee. Jack was forever running around topping off his customer's coffee cups and chatting. It's a good thing the chef helped put food on the tables or all would have full coffee cups and no eats.

Todd was anxious to talk to the three fishermen who were one of the night crews and asked, "Hey, guys, how was the action under the Light?" Eric popped his head up, "Hi there, Todd." And then in a very hush-hush tone he continued, "We killed them. We had fish near three hours and the water was full of peanut bunker. With that bait around, you can't miss. Mike and Tom both slammed twenty pounders and I picked a thirty one pounder on a black darter. High water fishing rip the first three hours of incoming is the best adventure in Montauk!" Holding his coffee cup up again for a refill, Eric went on, "Todd, where the hell have you been hiding yourself, no one has seen you on your tabletop rock for weeks?" Todd answered simply, "It's called family business, boys." "Okay, okay, Jamie was giving me those wifey stares and grumbling about the late fishing hours I've been keeping. When you guys get married you'll learn how the missus can cut down on your freedom. They have an agenda; it's called family. You have to know when to give and take. It's like fishing, guys. Last week it was give, this week it's take." They all laughed including Jack, holding his coffee pot up high, standing next to Todd. Jack never missed out on good gossip. Todd said, "Later, boys, it's me and tabletop tonight!"

Chapter 14

The stick Todd designed and built for Clive was extremely durable and water resistant. His first step was to make a unique blank with the highest quality graphite cloth available. He used a multi-dynamic blend of advanced high-modular graphite for maximum durability and sensitivity. The he added powerful and substantial mid-modular graphite and finally an outer wrap of multi-directional woven graphite cloth in a fine weave for superior strength. Todd gave the tip section a layer of advanced F glass to enhance performance and proper tip action. He chose the highest quality Fuji components for guides, tip top, reel seat and gimbal and used tapered hyphon fore-grips and utilized a diamond wrap.

Todd's love of fishing lured him into the art of rod making. It was just a hobby; nothing serious, he never put any demands on himself. He also liked fly tying; the local fishermen never had enough of these. His creative nature was apparent in his line of fishing goods. Each rod or fly he produced was a love affair and the feedback from his customers gave him pure enjoyment. He was not competing with the two village tackle shops but rather just having fun honing in on his fishing art.

Orders were filled at Todd's leisure and his market was limited to the local fishermen. Paulie and Johnny, the village tackle shop owners, knew it was only a hobby and harbored no ill feeling toward Todd. In fact, Todd bought his supplies from both of them and would confide in them whenever a problem arose. Todd's customers were his fishing buddies and understood he had a family to watch over and a business to run but the seduction of fishing was in his blood like the rest of the locals and the guys were patient.

When the word came that fish were in via the cell phones, VHF radios or word of mouth, half the town would hit the beaches. What a wonderful, exciting sight to see; fishermen, lined up like little toy soldiers, shoulder to shoulder, casting into the boiling water as hundreds of fish swam colorfully, erupting out of the waves, exploding, chopping and cutting away at their lunch in a berserk, ferocious, turbulent frenzy! It was grand to see this surging uproar played out fifty feet from the beach; thrilling, down right fun! It was the best medicine for stress and whatever else bothered you. There they were, yelling, shouting at each other; big smiles on their lighted- up faces. They were young again, like children on the beach with no cares in the world, just having a fun day.

Montaukers are a unique people. For one thing, their homes lie one hundred miles out into the Atlantic Ocean. Amazing events happen along their beaches. The waters are full of strange, spooky and unknown treats. Talk about the "White Lady of Avenel", anything is possible in Montauk. It was a given that most of the locals had eerie encounters along the shore, especially at night.

Todd double checked every aspect of Clive's new stick; satisfied and pleased with his work. He held her with great expectations. You could say, he was "chomping at the bit". Gently and ever so gingerly, he raised her into the air like a new born. She was so light but he could feel her power oozing into his hands. He felt her soul shining through the graphite rod butt. His spirits were high with glowing enthusiasm that he exclaimed, "My God, what have I created here? It's time to try this beauty out!" Catching himself, he thought, at first go easy, experiment with a few short casts;

warm her up, Then tease her to a few medium casts, get a better feel of her, then, and only then, will I start to unload her!" It was a love affair and Todd knew just how to handle this baby. He left the rod room, waved to Craig and called, "I'm going to sea test this baby. Be back within the hour." Todd went out the back door, jumped in his truck and headed for Fort Pond Bay.

Craig was six feet tall and twenty pounds over-weight. At lunch time and after work he would go to the Montauk Play House where he would work out in the new state of the arts gym. Everybody liked Craig. He had an engaging personality and was always in a good mood. His bright brown eyes matched his curly brown hair. As an expert angler and cook, he was forever trying to find time to hit the beaches like the rest of the busy locals and to try out the many fish recipes lying on his kitchen counter. Craig was particularly pleasing with the customers, using his humor and making them laugh.

Clive came in a half hour later and gave Craig the "hi sign", saying, "Hey, Craig, where's Todd and my new toy?" Grinning, Craig answered, "He's out to sea in a little pea green boat testing your rod." They both laughed at Craig's corny joke. "Give him a few minutes, he'll be back. Meanwhile, grab yourself a fresh cup of coffee, Clive, I just made a new pot." Craig pointed to the mound of round, white sugar-donuts, "I made them myself this morning and they're going like hot cakes. That's why I'm off to the gym again today." Clive helped himself to the goodies and sat down in Todd's wicker chair. Looking out the front window, he could see the birds, every so often, picking up the bait in the ocean. Noting the action, he said, "It must be sand eels. Looks like slim pickings but according to Jack, it was good last night but slow this morning." Clive and Craig shot the shit about fishing and football.

Todd returned through the back door, beaming cheek to cheek with one of the outrageous, self-praising braggadocio smiles that said it all. He handed the stick to Clive, 'You owe me double, buddy, this rod casts a mile and I used only a two ounce buck tail! The good Lord only knows what will happen when you put on a three ouncer! You might even hit Block Island!" They all laughed a good laugh. Todd assured Clive even more, "When the fish are out of range, by one or two casts you'll be the only one to reach them. This is not another stick, it's a cannon! Why, shit, I'm going to build one for myself." Not to miss out on the action, Craig interjected, "I want one, too!" "You're on, Craig; we can do the lay away plan for yours." "Thanks, boss," Craig answered happily.

Todd and Clive walked back to the rod room. Closing the door, Clive said, "Todd, thanks for making up the stick but more importantly, did you read your bible today?" Todd took the rod from Clive and placed it gently on his fishing table. "Sure did, Clive, Luke Eight; Jesus was teaching me about planting. The good seed is the word of God and I'm not going to throw seed onto stone or into thorns." Clive straightened up, "Good, son, remember this; there's more to life than fishing." Todd shook his head in agreement, "Come, I will make you a fisher of men." Clive was so impressed with Todd's studies and diligent bible reading that he clasped Todd's arms and almost gave him a bear hug. "You got it, Todd, the book is man's freedom. Fishing is joy but the whispering of Christ's joy was humbleness in that manger. My dear friend, remember always to be humble." Clive continued on, "You have an awesome family and you built your business from scratch. Hell, I recall when you were just starting out, why you had mortgages up the ass. Now, you're clear and free of that. You have worked hard and one day, Todd, you might bring your kids on board is they're so inclined. The good book is the true measure of a man's life." Todd was amazed how intense his friend was and with his vivid, luminous eyes, radiating with such dazzling power, he felt that Clive had "the light of heaven within him".

Chapter 15

No sooner had Todd unlocked the liquor store's door, Craig, popped in. "Good Morning, Todd," and enthusiastically said, "last night at Scott's we killed them!" He went on to mention there was no room under the Light so they hung out at Scott's. "I picked a seven pounder and Cathy pulled a twenty four out. We had fish for two hours and we didn't even have to stand on those spooky rocks trying to gaff our fish down in that rough water. Damn, Todd, I'm getting too old for that shit. Just standing up on those cliffs hurts my knees and gaffing those cows is dangerous and back breaking shit. We were standing in our waders, water up to our asses and there was no fear of falling or stumbling down into the abyss. Sure a lot of fun pulling fish in comfortable surroundings." "You're right on; it's starting to get to me, too, Craig. I might be joining you and Judy at Scott's pretty soon." They both had a good laugh as Craig said, "Yeah, that'll be the day. You fishing at Scott's? Shit, you're a landmark up there. One day we'll put a plaque on tabletop, THIS WAS TODD'S ROCK." Todd smiled, "No plaque for me, Craig, I'm going to buy a twenty eight foot Acquasport outboard and name her "Lazy Bones III" and sit in my white wicker chair, picking flounder." Craig offered, "Yeah, Judy and I will bring beer and sandwiches and bait." "Okay, Craig, sounds good. Look, I'm going in the rod room got to finish up Clive's rod. I expect him in today. `If you have any problems, you know where to find me." Todd walked off to his make shift rod room in the back of the storage area.

Stuie called Craig on his cell phone, "Hey, Craig, I went out on my boat today, checked out the bait along Gin Beach, Shagwong and up to the Light. There's a shit load of bait, it's a mixed bag of sand eels and bunker, right up on top all along the shore line. You'll kill them on the incoming under the Light. Don't miss out, Craig, I'm telling you, bub, it's going to be a killing up there! Don't say I didn't warn you. Tell Todd, I think he's also heading up front tonight. I can't make it; my damn back is killing me; my shoulders hurt like hell. I must have raked close to twelve hundred clams today. Mom said to take a good hot bath and she's going to heat up some linseed oil and rub me down. I got to get a good night's rest and lay off tomorrow.

Shit, Craig, I'm starting to feel my age. Take care, bub, see you at Jack's tomorrow. I can't wait to see that fifty pound cow you're going to pick tonight! Catch you later, buddy." "Thanks, Stu, I'll catch one for you!' "Okey, dokey, Craig."

Craig went on the internet and found the Montauk/Block Island Tide Table. Incoming would begin at 7:00pm, the rush would take place about 8:30 and high tops off at 10:00-10:30 depending on the wind. Perfect, he thought eagerly, I can go up front right after dinner. Damn, Judy is waitressing tonight at Dave's. She'll miss out, shit, if I get a big mamma, Judy's going to be really pissed and I'll have to hear her crap all week. She's one of the best fishing women in Montauk and her competitive spirit hates missing out on the big bang. Oh well, that's life.

Todd walked in with their hot soups and sandwiches. "Lunch time, Craig, eat while it's hot. You going to the gym today?" "I was thinking about it but Stui just called me, there's a mixed bag of bait all along the shore line from Gin to the Light. He's one on the best baymen in Montauk, you know, and he smells fish under the Light." "I just heard that from Joe. I met him at the deli, shit, how does this shit get around so fast?" "Stu just called ten minutes ago." 'You know, they're tight, he probably called Joe before you." "Right, he probably called Charlie, too." "Probably."

"Are you going tonight, Todd?" "No, Craig, I can't make it. Jamie became nauseous at work today and left early. You know, with the baby on the way, woman's bodies go through all kinds of shit. Damn, I'm glad I'm a man, Craig. So, tonight I have to play Mom, get the dinner ready and help the kids with their homework. What about Judy? Can't she go with you?" "No, she's on at Dave's tonight. "Well, I know for sure that Clive and his cannon will be there." "Yeah, you're right. I'll go up after dinner. By the way, what are you cooking for dinner?" "I'm not cooking; Jack's roasting a chicken, doing mashed potatoes and vegetables. When I put the food on the table and wake Jamie, shit, she's really going to be surprised." "Oh, that reminds me," shuffling through his pockets, "here's the recipe you wanted for beef barley soup. Remember, use a T-bone steak. That's the secret to my soup! People are cheap and don't want to buy a good steak for soup; they buy that cut up stuff; it's crap. The bone adds a real bouquet to the soup. Oh, and use some water, I have it written down and three quarts of chicken broth. That's also the kicker. Shit, I can taste it now. It's damn good soup if I say so myself! It was Mom's recipe. She got it from her Mother." Todd looked at the recipe quickly, stuffed it in his pocket, "Thanks, buddy, I'll make it tomorrow, but now, let's eat lunch!"

Craig pulled into the upper lot at the Lighthouse noting that the moon was three quarters full; good, plenty of light to work under. He got out of his truck, put on his waders, jacket, wader belt, carried his gaff and tackle bag, grabbed his stick, secured his truck and started down the path leading to the rocks under the Light. It was 7:30pm and a number of vehicles were in the lot besides his. Good again, he thought, I hate going up on those rocks by myself; they're spooky. Hopefully, tabletop, one of the safest and flattest rocks, would be available. He walked through Scott's and with some difficulty managed awkwardly to climb the rocks. Between the moon and the Lighthouse beam, he was able to clearly see his way to the top. Great it was vacant!

Over the years, Craig had lost some of his coordination but his knees were working smoothly and he felt strong, thanks to the gym. Okay, he focused on his target and reached it; safe at last. I'll just take five and catch my breath; no hurry, he mused, will wait for the stronger and faster currents to entice the fish to come in. He could make out about ten other anglers working the rip, casting out buck tails and plugs into the water. He thought, shit, I'm damn lucky; they must all be locals leaving tabletop for Todd. What a respectful bunch of guys. Okay, good again, things couldn't be going better.

Craig heard footsteps approaching. He turned, "What the fuck?" Stu, announced, "Yeah, yeah, yeah, I'm here. Went and got a massage, sat in the Jacuzzi for an hour, feel great, bub. You really didn't think I was going to miss out of this!" Stu passed by Craig to his post. Craig readied himself and took his first cast using a black darter. He thought, if Eric got that cow on his black darter, why the hell can't it work for me?

After an hour of casting, Craig broke out his thermos, poured a cup of coffee, raised the cup to his lips and was just about to take a gulp when he heard something. Startled, he swung around to get a better bearing on where the noise was coming from. Then, more alarmed, he heard heavy footsteps moving closer, together with a strange, creepy, dragging sound. What the shit? He started to panic! It's getting nearer, zeroing in on me! Damn these rocks and damn that creepy noise. If only Judy was here I wouldn't be so uptight. Suddenly, the moon ducked behind the clouds. He hated the darkness. The Lighthouse was losing its light now due to the surrounding mist. He raised his rod and took a defensive posture as the footsteps came closer. He could barely make out a figure. Squinting to see better, he called out, "Damn, where the hell is that moon?" All at once, out of the blackness, came a soft voice, "Hi, Craig, it's Cathy; sorry if I spooked you." As if on cue, the moon burst out from behind the clouds, lighting up Cathy's majestic face. Craig felt a great relief; the tension left his body.

The moonlight was bouncing off her prize fish; the silver beauty with its black stripes seemed to be dancing in the moon rays. Craig eyed the fish closely, "I'll guess she weighs thirty pounds!" "Close," Cathy answered, "my scale puts her at exactly thirty five pounds. She's almost bigger than me. Her tail was smashing on the rocks. Guess I sounded like the grim reaper," she laughed. Craig noticing the black darter on her stick remarked, "Looks like the black darter is high hook for the night. What time did you catch her?" Cathy glanced at her watch, "8:45, I always mark the time when I hook a fish." She held up her hand, "I had a bigger one and lost it, damn those rocks down there. She cut herself off before I could gaff her. Got to get this beauty home, Craig, I'll see you tomorrow at Jack's." Craig asked, "Just us locals here?" "No there's some big guy standing on turtletop, looks like this is his first time. He has lousy coordination and swings his stick like a real "googin", you know, must be some asshole from up island who doesn't belong here. When he saw my fish, I thought he was going to kill me. He just kept tapping his foot up and down like I stole his fish. Fuck him! Stay clear of him, Craig. He might be on drugs or turkey, you never know with those jerks from up island. See you, Craig; I've got to haul this baby up to the truck, not looking forward to it, oh well." Cathy lifted her beauty off the rocks and swung the rope once again over her shoulder.

As Cathy walked west to Scott's the moon darted behind the clouds again. To Craig's irritation he heard that unsettling sound once more. Shit, he thought, it is definitely weird here tonight. He missed Judy and knew she would be pissed when she learned that Cathy out fished her again tonight. Smiling to himself, he planned to make Judy a roast duck dinner with all the trimmings tomorrow night. That should take the beast out of her! The moon's sudden reappearance gave Craig the opportunity to catch sight of the big bulk of the guy down at the end of the line. Okay, he thought, I'm far enough away from that asshole, but, heeding Cathy's warning, he decided to keep an eye o him.

"Everybody's hooking cows but me," Craig fumed, "what the hell, tabletop, you were always good to Todd; give me a damn fish too." This is bullshit, the black darter works for everyone else, why not me?" His dashed hopes were turning into gloomy desperation. "I can't be the laughing stock at Jack's tomorrow. Could it be I'm at the wrong angle if the rip? Maybe that's why they call this fishing, not catching." He looked at his watch, "Okay, it's only 9:15, plenty of time before high water. Just relax; your cow is swimming out there somewhere."

Concentrating on his fishing once again, he never heard Stuie return. Stu had to call out, "Was I right or was I right? Shit, Craig, we baymen can smell fish, alright," holding up his thirty pounder. Craig looked to his right and saw Stuie and his fish in the bright moonlight. "Wow," nodding his head, "nice fish, Stu." His buddy smiled and said joshingly, "It's all in the hands, Craig. Play your darter like a buck tail. Shit, not everybody is gifted." Laughing, Stu offered to give Craig a few lessons tomorrow. That's all Craig had to hear. He exploded, "Fuck you, Stuie! I've been fishing while you were in deep water in your Mom's pouch." Stuie slapped his fish and laughing, called back, "I'm going home early, big guy, with my fish. Hope you don't get "sweet pickled" tonight!" Craig was about to blow up again but Stuie's laughter was so contagious that he slapped his rod and had a hardy chuckle, too. "Buddy, you know these guys down at Jack's will never let you live this down. They'll ride your ass to death." They both burst into stitches of laughter. "Stu, I'll see your ass at Jack's tomorrow and we'll see who the man is!" "Okay, okay, tomorrow, and I want to see his tail, buddy. We'll make a comparison and see who picked the bigger fish." Both nodded and stared each other down. "Okay, later, Craig, it's been a long hard day." Stu headed west with his fish on his back; swaying back and forth.

Craig cast out again, thinking, okay, I'll play her like a buck tail. Like on cue, bam, he hooked his first fish but could tell by her pulling action she was within the twenty pound class. Swell, but not what I'm looking for and brought her into the rocks, lowered his rod as he spit the plug and vanished. Digging his cleats into the surface of the rocks, he felt hopeful, "Okay, Stuie, I'll just swim her like a buck tail."

It was 9:30pm, the best of the rip, Craig knew. He cast out again, sure of another strike. While he was reeling and expecting an explosion on his plug, all of a sudden an arm grabbed his shoulder. "Hey, fella!" Craig jumped back a foot and looked into big guy's eyes. "Damn, don't do that again to me ever! It's creepy enough up here. I don't need to be scared shitless." Clive laughed and held his forty pounder up. "Craig, look what Todd's cannon hooked me! Helen's going to love me tonight! So, Craig, how are you doing?" "I just threw back a twenty pounder. Damn, I need something bigger if I'm ever going to even try to win the local tournament." "The tournament just puts pressure on you," Clive explained, "and takes away from the joy of fishing." "Hey, I see you were using a swimmer, Clive." "Yes," pointing to his plug, "I made it myself; that's the best part of fishing. It's homemade and I out hook those expensive plugs." Craig shook his head, "Damn, Clive, one day you have to teach me. I really would like to master plug making." "Okay, son, call me anytime," and winking at Craig left and headed for his truck. What a perfect night, conditions are at their best; the rip is loaded with bait and fish, thought Clive. Why, hell, you can't fail to get a large cow under these circumstances. Maybe Craig should say a prayer; it always helped me, he reminisced.

Just as the moon popped out again Craig surveyed his surrounds. "Shit, I'm alone, except for the big guy on turtletop rock. He's still there just looking at the sea. Where the hell is his rod? What an asshole! Like Cathy said, he's probably on rugs or turkey. Keep you eyes on him! Guess the other guys took their fish up the hill."

Focusing again on fishing, Craig called out, "Come on big guy, it's getting late and damn creepier out here." Ten more minutes and I'm going home to Judy, he decided. He worked his plug back to the shore line and the lure exploded; the line singing off. His heart started to pound. This is the big mamma! The fish was at full throttle, swam straight out then changed course, arching left. He judged her to be out about two hundred yards. Then abruptly she made a sharp u-turn and at full speed swam directly back at him. "No way, baby, am I'm losing you to this old bass trick," he yelled. He reeled and reeled up the slack, keeping his rod high at a twelve o'clock position; not giving this adversary a glimpse of hope. "Damn, concentrate, Craig, he's big and damn treacherous. Judging by his speed and pulling power I figure fifty pounds or better than what I call a tournament winner! Damn, slow down, big guy," gripping his rod tighter. Suddenly, he felt her arching right; then she turned straight out to sea, bent on getting her freedom. "She's going to try and strip my spool." Out close to two hundred and fifty yards now, Craig envisioned her exploring her possibilities and probing his abilities. "Go for it, big guy, put me to the test: this is what separates the men from the boy's." Craig felt panic starting to creep into his mind; then yelled to himself, "relax; keep concentrating." The line slowed down at last. "She's getting sluggish, she's tiring down after three runs, spent of energy as they say." He sensed it was time to ease her in and reminded himself to start hauling, little by little. "Damn, if only the moon would come out again from behind those lousy clouds. I need that light!" She was coming closer now as his line was spooling up. He shouted at the moon, "come on out, I need your light to help me climb on these hellish rocks and gaff her!" All at one, out of the darkness, a blow ripped the back of his head. He started falling, wide eyed; watching his rod slip out of his hands. The beast pulled his rod down into the rip. It was lights out.

Craig fell into a deadly, bitter sleep. The stranger caught him before he slammed his face into the rock; no bleeding please, and yanked him up on his shoulder. He climbed the embankment and put Craig into his tailgate, throwing a canvas over him. The stranger said, "Good, no witnesses." He was stimulated almost more than his flesh and blood could bear! He felt the pleasure of death.

Chapter 16

Judy pulled off East Lake Drive onto their driveway and noticed that Craig's truck was not there. She
felt hurt, annoyed and almost angry. Where the hell
is that man? He told me he would be back early; it's
11:00pm. Damn, what's, he up to; another woman?
No way, not my Teddy Bear; he's so sweet, a tasty cook
and a great lover and he's so damn reliable. Besides,
Jim our jewelry store guy whispered into my ear last
week and told me Craig had picked out my engage-
ment ring! He even put a down payment on it; going
to use the lay away plan. Oh, I love that man. He's so
kind and he's always making me laugh. Jim even mentioned he wrapped my ring in a box with pink paper
and a gold bow; so perfect! Tomorrow is my birthday,
she thought fondly, crossing her arms across her broad
chest: "no flowers for me!" Judy closed her eyes and
imagined that brilliant shining stone sparking on her

finger. She reminisced about them meeting a Scott's and how they were both fishing the outgoing as the day was on the decline. The sun, a radiant glowing red ball, was setting over Gardiner's Bay and Craig told her that naughty joke. They had been together ever since. Excitedly, she shouted out, "We'll get married standing in the water at Scott's!"

She got out of her SUV finally, walked up the path and unlocked the front door. The Cutty Sark bottle on the bar was just the ticket she thought and she poured a stiff drink. Yawning, she lighted a cigarette and sank back on the squishy couch pillows. Judy loved her job but it was hard, tiring work. Carrying her drink, she walked sleepily to their bedroom. "I know my Craig, he and Todd are probably killing fish. Those little boys, that's all they think about; they have Peter Pan's racing about their hearts! They're god fearing men! Good night, Craig dear; my soon to be husband, I love you," she said as she undressed for bed.

At dawn, Judy rolled over toward Craig's side of the bed and whispered, "How was the fishing, loverboy?" There was no answer. She opened her eyes wide with terror; not seeing Craig next to her. She jumped out of bed and raced to the shower. He was not there either. She bolted to the front window, pulling the curtains aside, no truck! Sheer panic grasped her as she ran for the phone.

In her frenzy, reaching for the phone, Judy, in her state of anguish, knocked it to the floor and burst into tears. She fell to her knees, hiding her wet face in her cupped hands and cried out, "Craig, oh Craig, please be alright." She crawled over to the phone, snatched it off the floor, opened it, scrolled down to Todd's number and pressed her send button.

Todd was an early riser. He enjoyed the first light. Their bedroom was bathed with those warm sun rays bouncing off the walls that reminded him of a ball-room with its luminous flickering lights. The sun was on the rise; a new day was dawning. The ringing of the telephone startled him. You know, that fear that wells up, when those real late night or very early morning calls come. He had a funny feeling as he reached for the receiver, noting that the night table clock indicated it was 5:15am. "Hello," he recognized Judy tear garbled voice. "Todd, oh Todd," she cried, "Craig's not here and his truck's not here." Todd sat straight up in bed and tried to concentrate. Clearing his throat he replied patiently, "Now, Judy, get a hold of your self, honey." Just then Jamie turned over and asked, "Todd, what's going on?" Todd put his hand over the phone, as he looked at her, motioning Jamie to be still. "Judy, did you have a fight?" "No, Todd, Craig didn't come back from fishing with you last night." "Judy, I stayed home last night. Craig was going to head to tabletop after dinner. Don't worry, he probably fished late into the night and slept in his truck." Todd's explanation eased her tension. "Okay, I remember him telling me he's done that in the past, before I met him." "Call him on his cell phone, Judy." "I can't. I'm using his phone. I'm supposed to get a new one today; mine went in the shit can." "Look, I'll be dressed in five minutes. I'll take a ride up there to check on him, okay, Judy?" "Thanks, Todd, you don't know how much that would mean to me. I'll meet you up there."

Todd turned to Jamie, "Craig didn't go home last night; he's more than likely sleeping in the back of his truck." Jamie said nothing. She just stared at her husband with a frightened, almost stunned look that only a fisherman's wife could do. Todd caught the stare, "Jamie, he's probably in the back of the truck dreaming of big fish. It was real calm last night and besides the rest of the guys was up there, too. If anything happened I would have gotten a call." Todd hopped out of bed, grabbed his clothes and hit the bathroom. Five minutes later he came to her side, bent forward, kissing her on the forehead and gave his reassuring smile. "I'll call you as soon as we find him, not to worry." He squeezed her shoulder lovingly and left.

Todd ran to his truck, started her up and took off with high hoped. He's sleeping in his truck that SOB. Boy, it's going to cost him a day's pay scaring Judy and me shitless! His flattering ass will be ours when we find him!

As he turned off Second House road, Todd put the pedal to the metal, as they say, increasing his speed to over eighty miles an hour. He figured he'd be in the upper lot in five minutes. As he flew by West Lake Drive, noticing no traffic on the road, he passed the ranch and considered slowing down due to the deer population but shrugged that idea off thinking, shit, Judy was in a state of panic. The deer were more numerous up at this end and over the years of fishing the Light he had seen countless dead deer, sprawled out on the sides of the road, tailless. The guys would cut the tails off to make homemade buck tail for lures. Todd had three sets of deer whistles on his truck; their high pierced ultra sound must be really screeching at 85 mph, he thought.

Arriving at the park entrance, he eased the brake, slowing up to a safe 40mph. and passed the first stop sign. Applying more brake pressure, he reduced his speed to 25mph. rounded the vacant ticket toll booth; then made a sharp right to the upper lot. Todd saw Judy waving her arms wildly. She started shouting,

"He's not in his truck, he's not in his truck," tears flowing down her red cheeks.

She fell into Todd's open arms and buried herself as he encased her tightly, leaning his head firmly against her warm, wet, face, his hands patting her back in a gentle way. She murmured breathlessly, ever so softly, "He's not in his truck." All of a sudden she raised her face from Todd's chest, looked to the heavens and with her mouth opened wide, let out a ghastly ear piercing wail, "Craigggggggggg!" followed by an eerie silence.

Lowering her face back to Todd's chest her body shook; she fainted. He lifted her carefully and put her in his truck's back seat. He used the water from his water bottle to wet a few paper towels and put them on Judy's burning forehead and around her warm neck. He waited for signs of her coming out of her fainting spell but it was all of two long minutes before she began to stir and regain consciousness. Whispering in her ear as he gently lifted her head, he said, "sip some water, Judy; it's okay, you're okay." She touched the bottle lightly as Todd tilted it toward her mouth, and locked her eyes on Todd. With a soft voice she said confidentially, "I've never fainted before." Todd, patting her head with a new cool towel smiled, "It's okay Judy, you're under a lot of pressure and besides, confidentially, I've never been in this position before either." They both managed to smile.

"I got to thinking, Judy, while you were out. Craig might have hitched a ride down town to Jack's with one of the morning crews." Judy was listening intently as Todd continued, "there's a chance he slept on his truck but when he woke up the truck wouldn't start because of wet wires and plugs. You know how damp the salt air is up here a night." Judy rolled her eyes in a thinking posture and looked back at Todd hopefully, "Yeah, there's just a chance!" As she tried to get up, Todd raised his hand but she pushed it away. "You know I'm a Montauk woman Todd, we're hard-assed, obstinate, industrious and difficult! It's bred in us from strong willed generations." Todd stepped back. "Okay, that's more like it." After she stood up, stretched a little, took off the towels and sipped some water, she put her hand on Todd's shoulder and said, "Thanks, Todd, but do me a favor and let's keep this our secret." Winking at her, "Judy, you got, it, my lips are sealed."

Judy glanced over at the Lighthouse and speaking in a taunting whisper and pointing to the structure said, "She's the safeguard of our men." No sooner had she uttered those words, she crumbled, crippled with pain. "Why couldn't she safeguard my Craig?" she gasped. Bending down and putting her head in her hands, she clutched her long red hair in desperation, thinking, Happy Birthday, Judy, that ring looks great on your finger.

Todd realized that Judy was worn to the bones and coming apart emotionally. He clasped her shoulders, "Judy, stop this, I'm calling Jack, you sit in the truck, now!" He moved to the back of the truck, out of listening range, and pressed Jack's number. After eight long rings, Jack's cheerful voice came on, "Good Morning, Jack's Coffee House." In a no- nonsense voice, Todd quickly asked Jack, "Is Craig there?" "No, Todd, what's up?" "Ask the guys, Jack, if any of them have seen Craig this morning." "Hold, Todd." Jack shouted above the noise and the chitter chatter, "Hey, guys, hold it," getting their attention. "Has anybody seen Craig this morning?" All stared at Jack, wondering anxiously what the hell was up. "No," shaking their heads and arching their shoulders. "No, no one here, Todd; what's going on?" "Shit, Jack, this is all fucked up. Craig is missing. Judy is heat-stricken and falling apart. I'm near panic. I think something terrible has happened to Craig. Got this horrible gut feeling, can't shake it, Jack, it's unnerving. Damn it, Jack, I fear the worst!" Jack heard the agony in Todd's voice, "what should we do?" "Nothing, damn it, do nothing, just wait for my call. Judy and I are going to tabletop. I'll call back." Click. Jack, still holding the phone to his ear, was alarmed. His eyes roamed from face to face and as he lowered his coffee pot slowly, he announced sadly to those nervous tight-lipped pondering faces, "That was Todd, Craig is missing." Eyes flinched, faces cringed; some grabbed their heads, others jumped up; at the ready to help.

Jack laid the coffee pot on the counter, raised both hands with fingers spread wide apart, "WAIT, don't go anywhere, they're up at the park. Todd is with Judy, they're on their way to tabletop, he's going to call us right back with his report. Just sit and wait. We'll have an answer soon." A troubled Jack poured coffee in his cup and sat at the counter, his head bowed.

The door burst open. All heads turned with great expectation, even hope. Wilton Kelley stepped forward, walking through the doorway, with his smiling face, gleaming white teeth and large brown eyes. A towering man of cheerful demeanor, he asked, jokingly, of no one in particular, "Does anyone know where I can get a good cup of coffee in this town?" Wilton's big laughing eyes scanned the room, looked at Jack and his pot on the counter, "What?" throwing up his hands. Jack said quietly, "Craig's missing." Wilton felt like he was just slammed with a shovel; "Craig, missing? When, where?" "Don't know, Wilt, Todd's with Judy, they're on their way to tabletop." "Shit, maybe I'll take a ride up there." "No. Wilt, Todd gave orders, just sit tight with us and wait for his call."

Todd took Judy's hand, pulled her up, "Let's go Judy." She didn't move, just stared. Tired and worn out she wanted to go to sleep. Todd started to walk, pulling her gently along. When they reached the cut, they picked up their pace. As the path became steeper, Judy's steps became slower but determined they reached Scott's Beach. They even ran east for another hundred and thirty yards to the rock under the Light. Todd helped Judy up on the rough, uneven, jagged boulders and they both walked prudently to tabletop.

Looking around, Todd noticed the seagull shit splattered all over the place. He saw the damn mussel shells all over the boulders that the seagulls drop like miniature bombs, breaking them open; another free meal for those feathery loafers. He surveyed their surroundings, searching for anything that might lead to a clue; any tell tail sign that would lead to Craig's whereabouts. Shit, nothing. Gazing down at Judy, he saw her foreboding stare transfixed at something down in the water. The sunlight lit upon a glittering shimmer of an object in the shallow water. He peered down and knew at once what it was. Like a mountain goat, he climbed down and retrieved the object. It was Craig's

Van Staal reel. Todd looked up at Judy. Judy yelled down, "Is it Craig's?" Todd nodded. Judy fainted.

Todd climbed quickly top side, administering to Judy. Shit, she's going into shock, he knew and ripped out his cell phone from his shirt pocked and dialed 911.

Chapter 17

The Montauk Fire House siren went off. Its eerie sound was disturbing to Todd. There were three long blasts followed by two short ones. The siren repeated, then silence. Shortly after, Todd heard a different whistle with a lower pitch coming his way. Must be the ambulance, he thought. Good, help would arrive soon.

Looking down at Judy, he saw that she was curled up in a fetal position. When she fainted she had landed on her right side, but, later, somehow, twisted on to her back. The right side of her face was bruised; red and swollen. Damn, Todd wished, if only I had some ice. Kneeling beside her, he took off his jacket, formed it into a makeshift pillow and placed it tenderly under her head. He could see that she was breathing in quick, short breaths. Stroking the side of her head, he could feel her soft, silky, smooth hair. As he watched her strained face, he prayed silently that this nightmare would end. "Craig, where are you, buddy?" he almost yelled. Todd could feel his own breath becoming more rapid as his chest heaved in and out in quick spurts. Time seemed to stand still but his thoughts were racing uncomfortably in his mind.

The screeching of the police cars' tires as they rounded the circle pierced through the air drawing his attention back to reality. He guessed it was the first responders and knew they were all EMT certified, just like Craig. He was part of the three man ambulance crew with Wilton, the driver and Mike, the team helper, who sat always in the front with Wilton. Craig sat in the inner body of the vehicle with the patient. All of a sudden it was unexpectedly quiet. The sounds became fainter.

Jack and the guys were alarmed and anxious as they listened to the distress signal. It was a more foreboding warning to their ears because of Todd's earlier call. The code, three long, two short was for the ambulance crew. Wilton's pager had buzzed prior to the regular signal. He bolted through the door as the siren wailed throughout the sleepy community and jumped into his truck, started her up, reaching over at the same time to turn on his green emergency lights. He thought, how utterly useless this is. Nobody on the road paid any attention to these lights nor gave a damn whether they were green lights for medical ambulance crews or blue lights for the fire fighters. Jesus, Wilton thought, if it were one of their relatives or friends, I'll bet they would move over and give the right of way. Wilton had long ago concluded that the only people on the roads should be the ones who really had somewhere to go and wanted to get there. Thrusting his foot on the accelerator, he moved out, ignoring the creeping paper delivery van.

The conversation at Jack's took on a gloomier seriousness. The guy's assumed the siren was for Craig. Like Pavlov's dog they all looked to Jack for guidance, solace and answers. Jack was at his best when problems arose. He had a degree in philosophy that came in handy when like a friendly bartender, who often doubled as a shrink, he listened intently and gave much sought after advice. Picking up his coffee pot and raising it up high, "The coffee and donuts are on me today, fellas." Their ripple of subdued laughter eased the tension. Jack also announced, "Let's all wait here for Todd's call."

The dispatcher, as usual, had given accurate information to the police. When they arrived; two cars, four cops, at the Lighthouse, they rushed down the path and on to tabletop. Todd, in deep thought, was surprised when a hand grasped his shoulder and a female voice whispered, "Hey, buddy, are you alright?" Standing above him were four uniforms with shining silver badges. He could see the concern in their eyes and on their faces. Todd managed to blurt out, "I'm okay, but Judy, here, fainted, hit her face on the rock. I think she's in shock." Officer Maureen O'Hara knelt quickly beside Judy, opened her medical bag, placed the stethoscope on the tip of her arm and took Judy's pulse.

While Judy was being attended, Police Officer Roy Thompson, a good friend of Todd's and a fellow surfcaster, asked Todd how he was doing. Todd shook his head as if to say, who knows? He asked Roy Thompson if he had some water. Roy handed him a bottle of Saratoga Spring. Todd took a sip, rinsed his mouth, spit it out and gulped half the rest of the bottle.

"Todd, I just notified Coast Guard, they're on their way." "Thanks, Roy." Taking out his cell phone, Todd called Jack. "Hello, hey Todd, what's happening?" "It's not good, Jack. Judy's down and we found Craig's reel at the bottom of the rocks in the low water." Jack stiffened, thinking, Craig was in the water, "Todd, what should we do?" "Tell the guys to get everybody available, hit the beaches, search every cove and rock formation. Depending on the wind conditions, Jack, and the currents, Craig could be anywhere. Tell the guys who have boats to scan the shore line. And Craig was wearing his sandy colored dry suit so he's not going to standout so tell them to get in close." "Okay, Todd, anything else?" "No, Jack, just get on it!" "Right, buddy."

Jack paused, tried to organize his thoughts. In a loud, commanding voice, "Okay, guys listen up. Todd found Craig's reel down in the low water at tabletop. Get every available body you can to search the beaches from Hither Woods State Park up to the Light. Check every cove including their corresponding rock formations. Eric, you and Jim start at the State Park, head west to Southampton. Craig was wearing his light sandy colored dry suit. Guys, keep a sharp eye out for him. Those of you who have boats scan the shore line on the north side up to the Light; then head west. It was outgoing water and depending on the wind and currents he could be anywhere from Block Island, Cartwright's or down west. Move out guys! Craig is out there in the water somewhere."

Todd felt guilty. "If only I had gone fishing with Craig, maybe this horror wouldn't have happened. But I had to take care of my family, they're my life, especially now with the new one on the way. Craig, please understand, I had to be home." Roy patted Todd on his arm, "better call Jamie, Todd." "Right, I just don't know what to say. Jamie and Craig go back a long way, Roy, he's the brother she never had." Todd opened his cell and punched in his number.

It was 6:15am, Jamie had not gone back to sleep after Todd left. Sipping her coffee in the kitchen, taking in the view of Fort Pond she, too, heard the siren. Praying to herself softly "please God let Craig be safe," she was jolted by the ringing of the telephone. She answered, "Todd how's Craig?" "Jamie, we found his reel in the water below tabletop and we're assuming he's in the water. Half of Montauk is out searching for his body. Coast Guard is handling Search and Rescue and coordinating with Marine Patrol, the Police and the Town Officials. It must have been a rogue wave, Jamie, it happens up here on occasion. It almost happened to me a few years ago and if it wasn't for Clive I might have been in the drink, too....." What are you saying, Todd?" "Let's talk about this later. All I know is Craig's missing; we're doing our best to find him. Judy fainted; she's in shock. The ambulance just arrived. I'll call you back." "Todd, be careful, don't do anything foolish, leave it to the professionals." "Right, Jamie, I'll call you later, keep you updated, okay?" "Okay." Todd closed his cell as he looked down at Judy observing that every so often her body quivered. This nightmare is just beginning, he thought.

"Todd, here come the ambulance crew," Roy announced, pointing to Wilton and Mike. Todd glanced up to see Wilton, his face taut and highlighted by the deep frown on his forehead. Mike looked frightened and followed Wilton awkwardly. He was strictly a beach fisherman and uncomfortable since he knew only the best fished from up on the jagged rocks. Wilton was all business and had a professional air about him as he nodded to both Todd and Roy then knelt down next to Officer O'Hara to discuss Judy's condition.

After completing his check list Wilton motioned to Mike to bring the board. Two of the officers assisted Maureen and Wilton; all four eased Judy carefully on to the white back board securing her fragile body with spider straps. Wilton attached the head and neck pads, and deciding that Mike was incapable of handling the board, signaled to Todd who he knew was sure footed, to take up the rear. Together they lifted Judy up, taking cautious steps and walked back to the awaiting ambulance.

Wilton slammed her into gear, hit the lights and the siren and moved out. Turing to Mercedes, who was substituting for Craig, he saw that she was watching Judy's vital signs on the screen. "How's she doing?" Mercedes an advanced technician replied, "Fine Wilt, just fine. Keep your eyes out for the deer!" "Okay, ma'am!" Mike sat quietly in the right seat, thanking God he made it off those life threatening rocks.

As soon as Wilton had completed backing the ambulance in to the emergency entrance driveway, Mike slid Judy cautiously out onto the awaiting gurney. "Call me when you're ready for pick up, Wilt. She's probably going to stay overnight." "That's what I figure, Mike. I'll give you a jingle as soon as I know what's going on. You and Mercedes head back. If you hear anything about Craig, call me." "Okay, Wilt, will do." Wilton followed Judy through the automatic doors.

Chapter 18

Walking through the upper parking lot toward Todd's truck, Roy spotted his friend ready to pull out. "Where're you off to?" "Jack's, Roy, that's where the control center will be. All the guys know to call Jack; keep us updated especially if someone finds Craig." "Todd, if I hear anything; you'll be the first to know." Good to have his buddy involved, Todd thought. Roy was a dedicated police officer. His 6'2" well built body looked impressive in his impeccably kept uniform. Yet, Roy had a boyish look and the brightest blue eyes that Todd ever saw.

Todd started up his truck, hesitated for a moment and called,"Hey, Roy, I have a real problem. You know, I was always one of those people who didn't care what happened to other people as long as it happened to them, you know, someone else. Now that something has happened to Craig, I feel ashamed and it's taken me down a peg or two. I can't believe I thought like that." "Hey, buddy, they taught us at the academy, in Psych 101, that everybody hopes it happens to someone else, it's called self preservation, buddy. We all have an aversion to trouble. It's natural human behavior. After twelve years on the force, I've become hardened to these situations. That's where my training kicks in. Trust me, Todd, the evil out there will never rule. It may try to make small inroads but eventually it is conquered." "Yeah, I guess, Roy, how about Craig's truck?" "If there's a crime or missing persons we impound it for forensic evidence and we'll take it back to headquarters. By the way, Todd, I need a complete list of the guys who were fishing last night with Craig. Make that your first priority. I'll need that list to conduct interviews. Better yet, you contact all the guys; have all of them meet me tomorrow at Jack's, 7:00am, sharp." Todd nodded, "I'll keep in touch and, Roy, thanks."

Roy walked back to tabletop to check the scene once again. As they taught him at the academy, don't overlook anything, look for clues directly around the scene and scrutinize any significant thing even if it may seem far too small. Use all five senses to find an item of interest. Nothing, Roy thought, no blood, no small items of interest, not even a cigarette butt or a match. This is not a crime scene, just a missing person, no need to photograph or videotape, he mused. He walked east, another hundred years; nothing. Returning to his car he told Officer O'Hara he couldn't come up with anything of interest. "Maybe, tomorrow the interviews will give us something, Maureen." He watched as the police tow truck hoisted Craig's truck up and once in place they followed it to Headquarters and filled out their reports. It was 7:30am.

Master Chief James Hueber's crew recognized the call from Officer Thompson at exactly 6:33am. Chief Hueber knew the drill for a person or body missing in the water. He'd been through it a number of times. With so many drunks driving, sailing or jet skiing, he automatically grabbed his MOB (Man Overboard) checklist. The Chief liked to think things out before he took action. He had to be a prudent leader given all his responsibility but this is where his experience kicked in. A muscular one hundred and seventy pound guy with a Coast Guard haircut, piercing brown eyes and masculine features, weathered by the elements, he was handsome, intelligent and imposing.

Checking his watch and knowing that time was precious; he walked briskly to the Control Room and gave orders immediately to get the chopper up and to begin the search and rescue mission. Next he ordered the launching of the forty seven foot cutter and the twenty eight foot power boat to the last known location of the victim. In between search and rescue operations his men drilled, practiced and rehearsed; they were ready under any circumstances. Once on site they would feed all known wind, current and way-points into the computer. At lightning speed the electronic brain would compute to where the most likely grid area was for them to stage their mission.

Chief Hueber telephoned Chief Edmond Michaels at East Hampton Marine Patrol. Michaels sent two of his twenty eight foot boats. Next Hueber filled in Chief Becker of the East Hampton Town Police and the Town Supervisor during a conference call. They responded accordingly and ordered police and town boats to join the search. Next on his check list he called, in order the: State Police, State Department of Environmental Conservation (DEC) and finally State Sheriff's Department. All responded positively.

As the morning dawned the water grew thick with crafts all searching for Craig. Between police boats, Coast Guard, local boats charter boats, official craft and a sprinkling of jet watercraft it appeared that every inch of water was carrying a ship. One had to wonder, was there enough water in the sea to hold up such a large armada? It was a sight to behold! Why, it was almost amazing to watch them jetting in and out. All wanted to solve the riddle of Craig's disappearance.

The search continued until one by one the boats were low on fuel or food. Coast Guard and Marine Patrol, well equipped to meet these eventualities, remained until nightfall. Both agencies searched the next day to no avail. After three days, the Coast Guard ended the search officially.

Roy had called Chief Becker the night before and they both decided that Todd should handle the interviews since Todd was extremely well trained in this area and his knowledge and experience could not be matched by anyone on the force.

Chapter 19

When Roy arrived at Jack's the next morning, Jack was pouring Todd a cup of coffee. "How's about it Roy, a cup of coffee?" Roy signaled with his thumb up and Jack, feeling that he was now part of the investigative team, poured him a cup proudly. That pot of coffee seemed to get Jack to all the right places. Roy sat down next to Todd, took a long sip, looked at Todd and said, "It's your show, bub, what should I do?" "Roy, I'm going to ask you to strip." "What the hell you say, strip?" "I mean it in the literal term, Roy. Take off your shield." "Why, Todd?" "It's intimidating and also lock your gun belt in the trunk of your cruiser." "Damn, Todd, where'd you learn this shit?" "How's about John Jay College Interrogation Technique 101? Trust me, Roy. In Jaws did Brody run around with his shiny badge on and pack a gun? No, he was unassuming as an ant in an ant hill. That's why he always got his man or in his case his shark." "Yeah, makes sense to me, Todd. I'll be right back."

Todd handed Jack a CD and asked him to put it in his stereo system. As Jack looked at it and read aloud, "Symphony No. 9 in D Minor," he eyed Todd quizzically and asked, "Are you serious, Todd? My customers will race across the street to John's!" Todd laughed, "It's a calming technique used by the CIA, FBI and Secret Service, Jack, when they conduct interrogations. You see, the person interviewed relaxes and sees things more clearly; with great detail and that's what we need."

Roy returned stripped. When he heard Beethoven's Symphony, he yelled, "So what the hell is this, another JJC technique, Todd?" "No, Roy," Todd answered quietly, "the big guys at CIA, FBI and Secret Service use this procedure. You'll understand as we proceed."

Todd began to arrange the chairs in a circle in the back corner of the coffee shop. Jack taking the words out of Roy's mouth, asked, "why a circle, Todd?" Again Todd, replied, quietly and patiently, "Because Jack, everybody is equal, everyone needs to be at ease and we're just going to have an open discussion on what may have been seen or heard. No good cop, bad cop foreplay."

The coffee shop door swung open; the bells tinkling, as the guys marched in like good troopers. Cathy drew up the rear. Todd noticed the discomfort but knew that Jack's coffee pot would soon take care of that. Cathy sat opposite Todd. Her memories of Craig had saddened her usually smiling demeanor. She was 5'9" and in remarkable shape. Dressed in jeans with a matching blue shirt, white sneakers and a pink baseball cap with her golden hair hanging down to her shoulders, she was an amazing, pretty, spunky girl with a gregarious personality who fished with the best and ran her own twenty foot boat. Cathy was a beauty with a tom boy attitude. Roy sat to the left of Todd followed by Eric, Mike, Gary, Stuie and Clive. Jack stood behind the counter refilling his coffee pots. He was well within range; not to miss a word.

"Okay, people," began Todd, "you were the ones fishing last night at tabletop under the Light so did any of you come up with anything odd or out of place?" Cathy raised her hand as if she was back in fourth grade, "What's with Jack, Todd, Beethoven?" They all grinned, shaking their heads back and forth. Roy glanced at Todd as if to say, this music is dumb, but Todd replied easily and looking directly at Cathy he said, "It's just a relaxing method to help us remember."

"Todd, I don't need Beethoven. I know what happened." "What would that be, Cathy?" "Well, I hooked the number two fish, Clive here beat me by five pounds," Cathy explained as she blew a kiss to Clive. All smiled including Jack with his fresh pot of coffee held high. Todd thought to himself, thanks Beethoven you're working. Cathy continued, "I spooked Craig, my fishtail was dragging on the rocks as I approached him in the dark. He was out of sorts with Judy, poor guy." Stuie interrupted, "I came by next; he was beside himself when he got a glimpse of my fish 'cause he didn't have one of his own. I gave him a fishing lesson, then left." Clive spoke up, "I walked right up to him without him knowing and tapped him on the shoulder and damn, man, he jumped back a foot, scared shitless." Cathy said, "That's probably 'cause I told him to keep an eye on the guy at the end of the line, he was acting funny." "What do you mean by funny, Cathy?" "I don't know, Todd, he just didn't belong up there." "What gave you that idea?" "Well, I noticed when he was casting he thrust his left foot forward as if to catch himself, you know, keep his balance." "Anything else Cathy?"

Beethoven moved to his next selection. "Nothing really Todd, no, nothing at all. The moon was shooting in and out and I was busy fishing, didn't pay any attention to him."

Todd put his hands together in his lap and stared directly into Cathy's eyes, "So you picked a thirty five pounder?" "Yeah, I had a larger one, in the forties, but he cut himself off the rocks before I could get to him, then climbing back up I saw the guy looking at me, maybe he wanted to help." "That's it, he just looked?" "Yeah, he went back to casting and so did I. Bam, that's when I caught my keeper and I was bringing him back up the rocks when the moon came out again and there he was holding his rod upright, looking and tapping his foot." "What foot, Cathy?" "What foot, shit if I know, I was busy with my fish, Todd." "Cathy, please try to think, what foot?" "Okay, jeez," screwing up her face; trying to recall. "Left foot, wait, let's think, yeah, it was his left foot and I just remembered he was holding his rod with his left hand. Okay, he was casting left handed and that's why I thought he didn't know what he was doing." "Do you think that he was pissed that you were out fishing him?" "Couldn't tell, Todd, he had his vest mask on, I had mine on, too. It was cool and pretty damp up there last night."

The guys shook their heads in agreement, muttering among themselves, "Yeah, it was cool; we all had our face masks on." Cathy elaborated, "I sensed that he was on drugs or turkey, you know those up islanders are usually on some shit especially when they come to Montauk; it's like a playground for them. Todd, you and Roy know what I'm talking about." "Yeah, Cathy," interjected Roy," we've seen it, it's normal behavior for those guys but the Montauk crew can hold their own, too, you know." "Yeah," snickered Stuie, "tell me about it." "Why did you sense he was on something, Cathy?" "Todd, any asshole, standing on a rock, holding his rod up high, tapping his foot, while everybody is hooking nice fish, has to be flying on something! I roped my fish and walked over to Craig and I mentioned to him to keep an eye on the guy, then I headed home."

Todd queried the others, "Anybody notice this guy?" All heads shook no except for Clive who said, "We're fishermen, not people watchers, Todd." Both Todd and Roy knew that when you fished under the Light you paid attention to only what was happening around you; the hell with anything else. It was dangerous enough to hold your own. Todd asked again, "Anybody have anything more to say?" Clive looked at Todd, "I do recollect he was using a conventional reel, you all know you have to be good and know your stuff to use one of those." They all agreed including Cathy. "Okay, guys, thanks for coming by. If you think of anything else, please drop by my store and fill me in." Jack asked if anyone needed a refill. All declined. They had to leave for work.

Roy asked, "What's your take, Todd?" "So he was perhaps on drugs or turkey; that's no big deal up there. Montauk's a party town. You know, half the guys that fish here are partying, letting loose in their trucks and campers. Besides, if he did Craig in he would have certainly taken his rod. That reel is worth six hundred dollars and the pole I built for Craig is another five hundred. No one in his right mind would leave eleven hundred dollars of equipment lying down on the rocks, right?" Shaking his head in agreement, Roy answered, "No way, Todd, if anything you would kill just for that gear." "Roy, write up your report and keep it in a special folder marked, uh, let's see, uh, mark it MTK the Disappearance." "Okay, Todd, I'll go back and report to the Chief while I'm there." "Have a good day, Roy," as he slapped him on the shoulder and as Jack, a foot away, said, "I agree, Todd, nobody would leave that pole and reel; eleven hundred dollars, I didn't know that fishing equipment was that expensive!" Jack felt he was even more of a team member now.

Todd's cell phone rang. He answered, "Oh, hi, Wilton, how's Judy?" "She's okay. Mike and I left her at her house and Mike filled us in on the search and rescue operation. Judy's parents called, they'll be here by noon. They left Virginia early this morning. The doctor prescribed a relaxant for her; she's holding up pretty good. Thank God her parents will be here. Todd any word on Craig?" "No, Wilt, it doesn't look like there's much hope." "What the hell, Todd? There's always hope!" "I hate to be the voice of doom, Wilt, but it's over twenty four hours with no sighting. It's like he just vanished. Wilt, everybody was out searching for a man or a body floating in his dry suit and nothing, Wilt. You know what the chances of finding him are." "Yeah, Todd, I see what you mean, okay, then I have another call. My Montauk Services is driving me nuts, too busy. I'll keep in touch, buddy. God bless you." Todd returned his phone to his upper shirt pocket, thinking, thanks, Wilt, we could all use a blessing now and then.

Todd gave a quick wave and walked out of Jack's. He spotted the four fishing buddies standing in a semi circle chatting. "What's up guys, planning to do some fishing?" he asked Clive, Stuie, Cathy and Gary. Stuie remarked, "As a matter of fact there's still a shit load of bait all along the north side of the Lighthouse. Tonight they'll be plenty of fish under the light. The water temperature dropped down a few degrees and if it goes any lower the bait might just move off so looks like it's now or never, Todd." "Can't make it tonight, guys; Jamie's off to bingo at the church. I have kid duty. "Too bad," Cathy added, "we're only going for a few hours, given the damn, sad circumstances, but, hell, what are we suppose to do, quit fishing? You know, we have lost men at sea and on the beaches, no way are we going to stop surfcasting. Shit, this is a tough and rugged fishing village. No disappearance stopped our fore fathers and it's not going to stop us." "Cathy, don't work your self into a rage," Todd said, extending his hand and patting her head softly. "It's getting late guys, I have to open the store; expect early morning wine deliveries. Catch 'em up, guys! Cathy is right; we all have to move on. I'm sure Craig would understand. He would stay out all night fishing if Judy allowed him. Good Luck tonight. See you all at Jack's tomorrow." Todd turned quickly and left. The others decided to meet at the upper parking lot that night.

Roy met with the Chief and informed him that the interviews resulted in a dead end. "Nothing, sir," Roy reported. As Todd requested, he set up a folder titled, "MTK, The Disappearances," placed a copy of his findings inside and put the folder in his bottom desk drawer file under D.

Chapter 20

There is only one road to the Lighthouse. The four fishing pals were racing along in anticipation of another exciting evening of fishing. Cathy was lead truck, Stuie right behind her. Clive was the third length behind Stuie and last was Gary whose truck toted a camper strapped to the back. Gary enjoyed the convenience of making himself at home after fishing, sometimes cooking up burgers and fries, and sharing beers with the guys. They had nicknamed him "pots and pans". He brought up the rear being slower and more cumbersome. All were chatting back and forth on their VHF radios; Stuie teasing Cathy, while Clive protected her like she was his daughter since he was the senior member of the group. Gary, the English professor, always corrected their English and grammar structure. All in all they were having fun, just behaving like mischievous kids, looking forward to a rewarding night, doing what they loved best, despite the recent events.

They parked their vehicles in the upper lot, put on their foul weather gear; without masks, and headed up front under the Light. After one hour of fishing, the cool breeze picked up bringing in that veil of moisture. It was dark yet the stars provided plenty of light, just like in a stage setting. Every once in awhile a star would twinkle as a passing cloud would dim its brightness; possibly resenting its intrusion.

He lay hidden in the beach grass like a deadly cobra watching and listening. He was thinking how cunning he was to have worn his military styled colored camouflage outfit. They were having one hell of a time, he thought, catching fish, releasing them, pulling more in and throwing them back. They were teasing and bantering among themselves who caught shorts and who snagged the big ones. It was like watching a comedic beach show. Their laughter irritated him. Nonetheless, the starlight, was perfect for him to make his move when he felt ready to execute his plan. Be patient, he told himself anxiously.

Clive checked his watch and announced, "I'm heading home, guys." Actually, he hated to leave while the fishing was this hot. "The playoffs begin at 9:30pm;

I've a half hour to get home. What about it, fellas, aren't you interested in the game?" Stuie nodded, "Yeah, yeah Clive, the bait is thick, we'll have to finish tomorrow, I suppose. Besides, it's going to warm up some tomorrow. That should keep the bait close to the beach." Gary agreed with Stuie, adding that he had a bet of one hundred dollars on one of the teams. All three brought in their lines. Stuie looked at Cathy, "Aren't you coming? I'll buy. We can go to O'Dooles. I'll even buy hamburgers and fries and we can watch the game." Cathy shook her head, put out her cigarette and placed her lighter and pack of butts in the inner ledge of the rock below her. She pulled her hand back on her stick. "I've got a thirty pounder at the end of this line, guys," her face lighting up, "take care, I'm going to spend a little more time up here. I'll leave at 9:00pm, bats and balls are no competition for this game!" They all wished her good luck.

He waited until he was sure they were gone. In an instant he was behind her. She never heard him or sensed his presence while struggling with her fish. She felt as though someone had put a red hot steel collar around her neck. At first she was paralyzed; dropping her rod. He lifted her off the rocks, almost two feet. Cathy was swinging her arms and legs helplessly. His forcefulness overwhelmed her. Cathy's neck snapped; the cartilage cracking like someone popping their knuckles. She collapsed. He felt she was limp. He turned her around looking directly into to her swollen eyes bulging out of their sockets; they were wide open; dull and lifeless. Her pale white face glowed cherry red. Throwing her over his shoulder like a bag of cotton candy, he was surprised how simple this, too, had been. He bent down, grabbed her rod and reeled in the line. He climbed the hill, scanned the parking lot and saw no one. Placing her in the truck, he covered her with the same canvas he had hidden Craig under. He drove slowly down to her truck, stopped, got her rod from the back of his truck and secured it safely to her roof rack. Not a bad looking stick, he thought, as he took off.

On Tuesday morning the raindrops seemed to dance to their own rhythmic slow beat as they splashed against the large front window of Jack's coffee house. Inside the talk focused mainly on Craig's disappearance. Jack was buzzing around with his coffee pot held high; half empty, smiling, chatting and seeking out the best gossip.

The conversations switched to the previous night playoffs. The Red Sox were going to play at Yankee stadium in two days. The baseball fans had plenty to say about it and they analyzed each play and scrutinized every move of the pitchers, catchers, batters and umps. These self-appointed sport's authorities rambled on pointing to the mistakes both managers made during some of the most critical parts of the game. If only they had been there, things would have changed for the better, they lamented.

Todd came in at 8:00am and joined Clive, Stuie and Gary. "Where's Cathy?" he asked. Stuie muttered, "She's probably asleep, she's on duty tonight, she usually sleeps late on her days on." Shaking his head, Todd added, "Yeah, a nurse's work is never done and I bet she's real tired after you all fished hard last night."

At Town Headquarters, Roy got a call From State Park Police Sergeant Steve Lubell. "Hi Steve, what's up, how's the family?" Steve told Roy he was going to be a father for the very first time. "I'm going to name him David, like out of the bible, Roy, he'll be strong and wise!" They both chuckled but in a serious tone, Steve said, "Last night, Roy, at 9:30pm I put a ticket on a truck in the upper lot. The truck's still there." Steve, are you telling me the truck hasn't moved?" "Yeah, it's weird; don't you think the person should have left by now?" Concern gripped Roy; another truck in the upper lot, what the hell is going on? "Roy, there's one other odd thing, there's a rod in the roof rack, it's not locked in, anyone could walk off with it." "Where are you, Steve?" "Right next to the truck." "Did you run the plate number?" "Yeah, belongs to a Catherine Mc-Coy." Roy froze hearing Cathy's name. As a possibility, Roy, asked, "Steve, she may be asleep in the truck, did you check?" "First thing I did, it's empty." "Okay, Steve, I'll be right there as soon as I can, have to see the Chief a minute, stay with the truck."

Although Chief Becker was in conference with his senior officers, Roy paid no attention to the "do not disturb" sign and walked right on in. The Chief glanced up from the pile of papers on his desk and smiled at Roy, "Hi, Roy, soon to be Sergeant Roy Thompson. Your appointment is tomorrow and I'm going to be very proud to hand you your stripes. You earned them, Roy, keep up the good work." Roy thanked the Chief; then informed him calmly of Cathy's dilemma.

The warm atmosphere in the room turned chilly. No one spoke. The Chief looked down thoughtfully; you could sense the situation was leaning heavily on his shoulders as his brow furrowed. The men there were all hardened law enforcement officers; their minds tended to focus on the negative. As the Chief stood up, he said, to Roy, "Take Todd up there with you, work with him and keep us informed." "Yes, sir," answered Roy, saluting.

The local papers carried the story on the front pages: CRAIG McCULLEY DISAPPEARED OFF THE MONTAUK LIGHTHOUSE, PRESUMED DROWNED, LISTED AS MISSING PERSON. The radio stations updated you every hour. The local community TV Network, Blum TV, sent their film editor, Abby Price. As usual Ms. Prince rushed out of the studio with her camera man in chase and ran to their oversized equipment van spending most of Monday filming Craig's scene. Now it was follow up time; more screen space with pictures that told nothing.

Chapter 21

Todd's cell rang, it was Roy. "Hi, Roy, what's up?" "Cathy's truck is parked at the Light, exactly where it was last night, according to Sergeant Lubell of the State Park Police. He ticketed it at 9:30pm. You know you're supposed to move down to the lower lot after 9:00pm." Fear gripped Todd. The guys saw the look on his face. "I'll pick you up at Jack's in two minutes, the Chief wants us to work together, be ready." In a daze, Todd said, "Cathy's truck is still at the upper lot; that was Roy, he's going to pick me up. Clive, you meet us up there, okay? It's important that you show us exactly where you guys were standing." "Check, Todd, I'm on my way," as he stood to leave. "Stuie, after work, come to my store, I want to interview you."

They all heard the siren in the distance. Todd handed his store keys to Gary who was now helping out. "Open the store as soon as you can, you know the routine, Gary." Jack overheard every word and lowering his coffee pot, thought, God, not again! Todd rose, turned to Jack, "I'll call you when I know something, break the news to the guys," and walked out as the police cruiser pulled up.

Roy's lights were flashing and the siren wailing as they peeled out from Jack's and headed to the Lighthouse. "Todd, Sergeant Lubell said there was a fishing pole in Cathy's roof rack, what do you make of that?" Putting his hand across his brow and shaking his head, "I just don't know, Roy, let's wait 'til we get there and get some facts. I don't want to start guessing, we'll know soon enough. You know, Roy, Cathy is one of the best fishing woman I've ever met; she doesn't make mistakes. There's no way she went into the drink, of that I'm surer in hell. There's something happening out there. I just can't a hand on it. Cathy is smart, Roy, never takes unnecessary chances, she knows the dangers of fishing under the Light. It just doesn't add up. There's something incomprehensible going on. I just don't know, Roy, I just don't know." They pulled up to Sergeant Lubell's rig just as Clive was coming to a stop, too. Super, he thought, I always wanted to follow a police car at high speed; that was great!

After the introductions, Todd examined the rod and recognized it at once; he had built it for Cathy's birthday two years ago; it was for her birthday, October 1st. Her fiancé, Bill, ordered it for her. "I remember that Todd," Clive said, "Bill insisted on gold letters, he being a jeweler." "We better call Bill, maybe he can shed some light on this," added Steve Lubell. All three looked at him uneasily. "Steve, Bill was in a car accident two days after Cathy's birthday," Todd informed him sadly. "Oh, jeez, I didn't know."

For starters, Todd slipped on a pair of gloves, popped the rod rack open, slid the rod out and turned it slightly. The gold letters glittered in the sunlight: Cathy McCoy, love, Bill. He examined the pole for any irregularities; nothing. He ran his fingers up and down the line; it was smooth and in good condition. Cathy used a two ounce homemade buck tail, he noticed. After unhooking the buck tail from the pole's eyelid, he turned and made a short cast onto the grass along the sidewalk. Speaking to no one in particular, "This conventional reel is an eight hundred dollar Van Staal reel, the rod nine hundred and the line sixty dollars. I fished with Cathy for two years, she never and I mean never let this pole out of her sight, especially after losing Bill. She held two things close to her heart; this rod and the gold cigarette lighter Bill gave her. Cathy is nobody's fool and I refuse to believe that she would leave her rod unlocked in the rack. No way am I buying that."

Swallowing hard, he continued, "We found Craig's rod down in the water, now we have Cathy's rod tucked neatly in her rack. This is almost totally unbelievable; same scenario we had with Craig. We have their rods and their trucks but what we don't have is them!" All three stared apprehensively at Todd. Roy interjected, "there is a possibility that her truck didn't start; maybe she got a ride home." "No way, Roy, she would never leave her pole." Todd was irritated; not with them but with the situation; it smacked of something bizarre. "Roy, this is not looking good. My gut feeling is that, she, too, has disappeared." Roy nodded, "I'm inclined to agree." Clive managed to say, "Oh, God forbid." Steve concentrated on the pavement. "Steve, you stay with the truck, Clive you come with Roy and me and show us where you guys were fishing," directed Todd.

When they reached tabletop, Clive pointing and walking explained, "I was here on Coppertop, Gary over here on Corner Stone, Stuie was fishing from Ledgetop and Cathy was here on her own rock, Mc Coy's, you know, her lucky rock. She had me put a shamrock under it awhile back." "Yeah, Clive, all the guys knew you did that for her," remembered Todd. "Is it still there?" asked Roy. "The shamrock? Oh, I guess

I should check," as he dropped to his knees, grabbing both sides of the rock. Something between the rock and the ground rubbed the side of his hand and as he peered down he saw a bright, shiny lighter. Holding it up for all to see, he felt almost sick inside as he announced quietly, "this is Cathy's twenty four carat gold lighter," handing it to Todd. Turning it over, Todd saw the inscription, "Happy Birthday, love, Bill". Todd knelt down to where Clive had found the lighter and sticking his hand into the ledge felt a soft object. He pulled it out and at once knew it was Cathy's brown leather cigarette case; four cigarettes were missing. "That's it, guys, Cathy, too, has gone missing," he said in a voice as hard as stone.

Roy and Todd searched the entire surrounding area to no avail. Clive was kneeling by Cathy's rock, quietly saying a prayer, when they returned. Todd walked over to Clive and asked, "Was anybody up here with you guys last night?" "No, we had the whole place to ourselves. Guess it was because of the playoffs." "You're probably right, Clive. Can you recall anything unusual, please think!" "No, Todd, we were just fishing, picking fish. It was really hot, Todd, like they couldn't wait to get on the hook. All that bait, damn, it was hot. Todd, are you sure she's gone?" "Looks that way, buddy. Anything else, Clive?" "No, I stopped fishing at 8:30, you know the game. Gary and Stu and I left.

Cathy had no interest in the playoffs. She indicated she was going to stay 'til; 9:00; then go home, get a good rest. She was on tonight. As we were leaving she hooked a thirty pounder. That's it, Todd."

Back at the parking lot, Todd reminded Roy to place a copy of his report in the MTK folder. The police tow truck picked up Cathy's truck and brought it to Headquarters. Roy placed the lighter and case in the otherwise empty evidence pouch. Todd and Roy stopped at Cathy's house on the way back. It felt very strange being there as they looked for any clues; nothing; dead end.

Roy dropped Todd off at his store. Just as he was about to open the door, Stuie pulled up and called to Todd. Todd walked over and leaned against the car's open window. "Stuie, Cathy's missing. I met with Clive at tabletop this morning. He explained you all fished and left early. Cathy stayed alone. Anything you can tell me, anything unusual?" Stuie had nothing to add. Todd walked back to his store, called Jack and informed him of this latest event. It was not long before the whole hamlet was talking about Cathy Mc-Coy.

Chapter 22

Chief Becker read Roy's sparse report. He looked pensively up at Roy and remarked, "Two disappearances in two days, two trucks two rods, two missing people; one male, one female and no indication that a crime has been committed. This is right out of "Rod Sterling's, Twilight Zone, Roy. We have no bodies, no witnesses, no phone tips, no weird letters, no sightings, no blood stains, no finger prints, no footprints, just a lighter and a cigarette case which belongs to one of the victims. Are you getting my drift, son? Good Mary, I've not seen a case like this. We turn up some evidence always no matter how small or at least a possible lead. We don't even have a pliable clue working." The Chief took a few deep breaths and continued, "in this day and age I would have thought to disappear without the slightest trace would be very unlikely. This is uncanny, Roy. I'm starting to see a profile of a serial killer among us!"

Roy was standing next to the office water cooler, sipping water, trying to digest the Chief's words. "Chief, what brings you to that conclusion?" Rolling his eyes, "This is how it begins, Roy. He taunts us but we can't find a clue." "You really think we've got a serial killer, Chief?" "Yes, Roy, I've studied cases over my years and this possibility can't be ruled out." "God, what are we going to do? How do we find him?" "WE don't, Roy, he finds US! He starts with cryptic letters, leaves peculiar drawings around, all that sort of thing. God only knows what this one will do."

"Chief, should we give the FBI a call?" "Hell, no, son, and be the laughing stock of the town? Roy, listen carefully, the department and I have a responsibility to the civilians of this village, and sure as I am Chief, that trustworthiness will damn well be upheld and besides," banging his fist on his desk, "if things go the way I fear they may go, the whole world may very well be observing and judging our performance. I have a reputation to live up to and that means so does our entire department. Now, I want you to take personnel, as many as you need, coordinate with Sergeant Lubell and Park Police and do a thorough search of the State Park and its surrounding areas. If possible, get even more locals involved."

Chief Becker, picked up his large coffee mug, took a big gulp, reached down and opened his bottom desk drawer. Taking out a new shiny set of Sergeant stripes, wrapped in plastic, and standing up like a proud father, handed them to Roy. "Son, we need the very best! Congratulations, Sergeant Roy Thompson!" Roy lifted his shoulders, stood erect, took the stripes and saluted his Chief. 'One more thing, call Todd, tell him I want to see him immediately."

Jim Becker was well into his fifties, 6'2', with short dark hair, silvering at the temples. Broad shouldered and trim with a ruddy complexion and eyes like a hunter, shaded by thick eyebrows, he exuded energy and moved like a cat, cautiously and meticulously. He was a man's man yet charmed the women with his Irish brogue.

"Top of the morn', Todd," gripping Todd's extended hand firmly. "Good morning, sir. Roy said you wanted to see me." "That's right, son. I've gone through your file." "What file?" "Hey, son, hold on, it's your military file and it's very impressive! A degree from John Jay College with full honors; First Lieutenant, six years with the military police, and sure, my lad, you took law enforcement courses at the CIA, FBI and Secret Services! By the 'laurels of my grand-pop', why aren't you one of us?" The Chief put his hand up, "I know, Roy explained it all to me. Told me your Jamie actually said, "it's law enforcement or me"." She sure in hell left me no choice, Chief. I decided to go with "me" and never regretted my decision nor looked back!" "Yes, Todd, she's a hell of a woman; a cut off her mother who I used to date in high school." "What happened, sir?" "Well I met Lily; she did me in, Todd, surer in hell if she didn't do me in! We graduated and married the same day. Damn, she makes an Irish stew that's fit for St. Patrick! Lily runs my life but I run my office so it's a trade off.

I guess you know why I wanted to see you, Todd. I could really use a good man like you." Chief Becker's face, reflected a disquieting seriousness, as he spoke, "I fear, Todd, that we are only seeing the beginning of more to come. I'm starting to wake up at night thinking about this case; something for me, that's never happened before. My missus said I need to drink a few Irish whiskeys before bedtime. Maybe she's right. Damn, I hate this strange feeling I have. Now, you, Todd, were born with an investigative mind. Please don't waste your gift, son. I need you. My staff is the best. I'm proud to work with them, Todd, they're good people and they work hard to keep the town's residents safe. They depend on us, Todd. Half the doors here are never locked and you know that says it all. Shit, these city folks have all those fancy alarms systems; for what? Every time their electricity spooks there goes their alarms and there we go. Damn, I hate the summer months of hell; nothing but accidents and alarms ringing." His brow furrowed even more and there was a sense of troubled urgency in his voice as he leaned forward, putting both hands flat on his desk, saying, "Todd, as a police officer for over thirty years, I've seen it all or at least I thought I had. But never anything like these two people vanishing off the face of the earth, so to speak. They have just disappeared. No bodies, no blood, no clues, no nothing. There's not even a shred of a motive. Two kids, enjoying fishing, under the Light; shit it doesn't get any better than that." He paused, looked down at his desk then peered up at Todd, with his haunting eyes. "Son, if my fears are proven right, we're in for one hell of a battle. Todd, I believe we have a terminator living among us and God help us if I'm correct!" The word terminator sent chills down Todd's spine. Not only was he stunned but the thoughts of his family became paramount. What the hell am I getting myself into, he wondered? The Chief read the look of anguish on Todd's face. "Todd, it's okay; we're all in this together; you're not alone."

Feeling as if he had just put his head into the lion's mouth, Todd, nevertheless, asked, "And what will my rank be, sir?" "Lieutenant, like in the Marines," answered Chief Becker. "No one will ever question your authority." They shook hands. "Let's keep this under lock and key, Chief, until I find some way to tell Jamie."

Todd returned to his store and asked Gary, "you fishing tonight?" "No way, Todd, not after what happened to Craig and now Cathy. All the guys I talked to are staying home and safe." "Good, Gary, no one should put them selves in jeopardy. It's too dangerous up there. We're all vulnerable. Night, Gary, thanks for your help and be safe."

Jamie was in the kitchen preparing dinner. As soon as Todd came home and hugged her, she asked, "Todd, what were you doing at Chief Becker's office today?" "How did you know I was there, honey?" "Linda, his secretary, I met her at the supermarket." "Jamie, the Chief wants to deputize me. He definitely feels I can be a major player in unraveling this mystery." "No way, Todd, I do not want you mixed up in this horrible thing. You have a family to take care of, Mr. Miller." The level of Jamie's voice increased as she continued, "No way, let the police handle this case, it's their problem, not yours." "Okay, Jamie, calm down; the Chief only wants me to be an observer." "What the hell is an observer, Todd?" she screamed. "It's someone who comes up with possible theories, gives advice, direction and I do have a gift for solving puzzles. Please Jamie, just this once, let me help, it's for Cathy and Craig." "You already have your mind made up; it's Todd's way or no way, the hell with the family!" "Wrong, Jamie, it's also for you and the kids." Jamie bowed her head and thought of her own vulnerability and that of Todd Jr. and Nancy's. "Get him, Todd, get the son of a bitch; do whatever it takes, but get him." She was shaking so hard but as Todd put his arms around her, she murmured, "I want to be there when the Chief deputizes you."

Chapter 23

Autumn gave Montauk back to its locals. The hectic whirlwind atmosphere of summer was over. Thank God, they're gone, cheered the villagers. The roads were no longer congested. There were no lines at the restaurants or the taverns. The stores were once again accessible. Why one could even pull up to a gas pump and get prompt service! The crowded beaches were sprinkled with more villagers, and of course, fishermen. One could play a comfortable round of golf without rushing a shot. Second home owners were heading back to their primary resident; their vacation homes locked up for the winter. Merchants breathed a sigh of respite along with everyone else. Fried nerves and bad attitudes faded away. Normality seemed to return to paradise; the party was over until next summer. Yet an inexplicable shadow loomed over the village.

The real estate business thrived in all seasons and as more and more people purchased their dream homes the summer population swelled. Since about a dozen real estate offices competed in this lucrative business, agents eagerly awaited the ring of their telephone, which more often that not, signaled the beginning of another sale or rental.

On this lovely fall afternoon, the telephone ring was so compelling that Sabrina, in her haste, cut off the second ring, which was against office etiquette, and, said quickly, "Beach Shores Realty, Sabrina speaking." "I would like to see the house your office has on Big Green Path," a deep male voice informed her. "Oh, yes," she replied, "it's one of our new listings with spectacular views of Lake Montauk." "Yes, indeed", he said. "I would really like to see it as soon as possible, are you free this afternoon?" Trying not to sound too excited, Sabrina answered, "Well, I think I will be free at 4:00pm, just let me check, uhm, yes, 4:00 is fine. Shall I meet you at the house?" "That works for me, Sabrina, 4:00pm it is," He hung up immediately. "Gee, I didn't get a chance to get his name or his number, oh, gee, well, he did remember my name. That's a good sign."

It was 3:30 pm and Sabrina knew it would take her about ten minutes to drive to the house and another ten minutes or so to turn on the lights and get everything set for her showing. As she picked up her notebook and slipped her purse over her shoulder, she waved to Ruth. "I'm going to the house now." Ruth smiled, "Good luck, honey. Make a killing!"

He walked one hundred yards along a trail called Glacier which led him halfway to the house. Continuing on through the thick woods, he arrived at the exact location where he had stashed the camouflage bag under a log two days before. The bag could accommodate a two hundred pound body. He sat down on the old, moss-covered, rotting log and thought how shrewd he was to have reconned this area. In this remote cul de sac all the homes were closed for the season. It was desolate and very peaceful here, he felt. From his strategic observation post he could watch her every move. What splendid isolation for him to work, he mused. He knew she would be all alone and defenseless.

He could feel his adrenaline pumping as he blue SUV rolled down the paved driveway. She's a little early, good, she's probably going to make the house look cheerful; brighten things up to make it more inviting for the customer. He watched her step out of her truck, walk over to the birdbath next to the front door, bend down and pick up a gray stone from among the many stones surrounding the birdbath, move up to the front door and unlock it. He thought how clever it was of the owners to hide their key in a fake rock. Watching her through the large glass windows he could see her open the blinds, put her purse and a book on the kitchen table and turn on some lamps.

Sabrina walked into the bedroom, drew back the drapes, allowing the gentle declining rays of sunlight to sweep through the rooms, chasing the gloomy darkness away. She turned on soft music; "a nice touch," she giggled. Walking back to the kitchen, she heard the doorbell ring. "Come on in, sir, I'm in the kitchen." As he entered the kitchen, he said, "Hello, Sabrina, I'm Sean O'Reilly," holding out his hand and grinning at her. Sabrina shook his hand, "Hi, Sean, have any trouble finding the house?" "No trouble whatsoever and she's a beauty. Love the landscaping, what a beautiful rose garden!" "Isn't it wonderful, you'll have roses almost all year long." She noticed the black rubbers covering his boots and thought, that's funny; it's not raining, oh, what the hell, just concentrate on the sale. "Just look at this view," she said to him, extending her arm in a sweeping motion toward the water. "You can see the entire harbor from up here."

The blow came from directly behind her, crushing her skull bone into her soft brain tissue. She staggered slowly then fell to the floor. Death was instant. He grabbed her limp body, held Sabrina upright and placed a plastic bag over her head, pulling the rip cord tight. No sense in getting blood or hair on the floor, he reasoned, let's keep it clean. He fetched the body bag from the front hall, placed her in it, zipped it, turned off all the lights and music, closed the blinds and drapes, locked the door and put the key in the pretend rock. He tossed Sabrina over his shoulder and began the hike back to his truck. After covering her body with the canvas he smiled.

Chapter 24

Beach Shores Realty's broker and owner Tony North stepped out from his private office into the main front area. Ruth looked up from her meticulous folders on her desk as Tony approached. "Let's call it a day, Ruth, it's ten after five. I see Sabrina already left." "That's the odd thing, Tony, she knows your policy; all agents are to report to you after a showing." He noticed the edge of concern in her voice, especially since he was an East Hampton Police officer, although now retired. "Right, so, what time was the showing?" "Four o'clock, Tony." "Where?" "Big Green Path." "Who was her customer?" "I don't know, it was her showing, she didn't say."

Tony sat down at Sabrina's desk, checked her calendar; nothing other than the address and time. He looked up, swung the swivel chair and faced Ruth. "We

163

were up there last Thursday, remember, it's adjacent to the County Park. All those nature trails are up there. It's damn isolated. Try her cell, Ruth." "I did, three times, she's not answering and that's what's worrying me. Her ID is indicating that I'm calling; Sabrina picks up always when I call her, Tony." Ruth took a sip of her lukewarm coffee; then stared down into the cup. Tony knew exactly what she was thinking. Flags went off in his head. He picked up the telephone and called the East Hampton Town Police. "Put me through to Roy Thompson, this is retired Captain Tony North." "Yes sir, Sergeant Thompson speaking." "Roy, one of my girls is missing." Roy stiffened, thinking the worst. "Tony, what do you mean she's missing?" "Roy, she went out to show a house up at Big Green Path, number 204. My office rule is that after every showing you return to the office and fill me in on the details. Sabrina has been with me for two years, she knows the rules."

Todd turned away from the chart he was working when he heard Roy say "missing" and picked up the conference phone. "Tony, it's me, Todd, fill me in, okay?" Tony repeated the reasons for his concern. "Tony, do you know who the buyer is?" "No, Todd, the agent's set their own appointments and then report all that to me." "Roy, do you have the address?" "Yes, sir." "Tony, meet us there and bring the keys." "That's a roger Todd, see you in ten." "What do you think, Lieutenant?" "Roy, there's one thing I know for certain, I don't know anything until I get the facts. Roy, when there are too many inconceivables, don't presuppose the bounds of possibilities until you have all the facts. Let's go, Roy."

When they arrived they saw Tony standing beside Sabrina's SUV, smoking a cigarette. Todd and Roy shook hands with Tony and could tell by the look on his face that his hopes of finding Sabrina were slim. They followed the retired Captain and stopped by the birdbath as Tony picked up the fake rock and took out the keys. "How clever," commented, Roy. Tony unlocked the door, swung it wide open, expecting the worst. All three looked around the large living room and then walked into the kitchen. They stared at the purse and notebook on the kitchen table. It obviously belonged to Sabrina. "That does it, Roy, we have another disappearance on our hands." "I'm glad I'm retired guys, but if I can be of any help, call me." "Tony, we'll have to check your phone records, maybe we can get a lead there." "Good thought, Todd, I'll call the telephone company first thing tomorrow. I've got a buddy who works down there, it'll cut the red tape; he'll get to it fast."

Tony wondered, "You know, guys, what's weird is that it looks like she never opened up the house, I mean, you know, make it more welcoming for the buyer." "We don't know that, Tony. Cathy's rod was replaced. The person could have closed down the house, maybe even locked it. We'll dust for finger prints. Sergeant, you handle that." "Yes sir, Lieutenant." The three officers conducted a preliminary search of the home; nothing. Tony locked the front door as Roy said, "Todd, Tony, I believe we can find a witness, get a vehicle description, even a plate number." "Roy, that's how they do it on TV. We have to think like him, let's recon that wooded area, spacing ourselves ten feet apart."

They were professionals; they knew exactly what to look for. Moving slowly along a south easterly course nothing seemed out of the ordinary until Tony yelled, "Over here, guys," pointing to a broken branch. "Good, Tony, he headed south down the hill, we're on his path. Let's go, fellas, and see where the hell this leads." Roy, call up Headquarters, get the dog team up here." Roy used his portable radio to make the call as they moved down the hill and came to another path where the sign read Glacier. Another two hundred yards placed them at a small paved parking lot. "I know this lot," Roy announced, "and that board over there describes all the walking trails." A disheartened Todd pointed to the pavement, "he parked here; no tire tracks but with some luck, just maybe, someone may have stopped by. It's a long shot but we have to follow it up. Roy, get on it immediately. Get a list of all the nature lovers who use these trails; interview them all. It's a small hamlet, Roy; everybody knows who uses these paths." Yes sir, right on it, Lieutenant."

Back at the Command Center in the room that Chief Becker had arranged for Todd and Roy to use as their Control Center and equipped with two desks, conference phones and a work table, Todd was coordinating two large charts; one a map with red flags indicating where the missing person was last presumed to have been, yellow for their truck locations and blue for any evidence found, a second chart exhibiting the person's ID, background history and other pertinent information.

Pondering his next move, Todd recalled his Shakespeare, "leave not a rack behind", believing he had read that someplace. "Think, Todd," said , aloud, "think like him , okay, we know he leaves his truck out of sight, blocks away from the scene, carries his victims to his truck, I think. He must be strong. Craig was about one hundred and ninety pounds, Cathy a light one hundred and ten and Sabrina, according to Tony, one hundred and forty. It appears he has no problem walking with his victims." Thus, Todd concluded, he must be clearly fit. He decided to set up another pro-file chart and titled it, THE FERRYMAN.

Todd proceeded to list what he knew to date: 1. he's fit 2. parks truck far from scene 3. knows where to find victims 4. he's smart; knows how to set up ambush 5. leaves no notes or drawings 6. doesn't take evidence 7. no time frame; day or night 8. what possible type work allows this freedom 9. what's the motivation 10. strikes with cunning aptness 11. has plan for victims 12. possible law enforcement; no clues 13. non-smoker 14. appears to surprise victims 15. uses remote areas

As he reviewed his list he realized some things he knew; others; he surmised. It was 7:30pm; he should be home with his family. Gary and Clive, working his shop, were a Godsend. Just as he was about to leave, Chief Becker walked through the doorway. A stone-faced Todd almost robotically briefed the Chief. The Chief said nothing. He stood staring at the word, FERRYMAN.

Four days passed since the last two vanished. Now the third disappearance hit the national news that evening. The residents, watching the pictures of the last known location, where the latest victim had been, saw the blue SUV in the driveway and listened attentively to every word the anchorwoman said. She spoke excitedly; spending fifteen minutes providing details of the car, the driveway, the house, and gave a definite description of the surrounding area as the cameraman flashed the scenes. For dramatic effect she held up three 20X20 color photos of each victim. The camera zoomed in for a close up of each smiling face. She continued babbling, but became more and more at a loss for words, since there was very little to report. There were no leads, no motives and no suspects. Her chattering stopped as she signed off and walked toward the blue car once again and patted its roof. As the cameraman adjusted to a wide screen view, she said, "This is Paula Martinson, be safe, until next time." The home audience was baffled. It was incredible how these news mongers would try to stretch a story for which they had so little material.

Montauk residents felt that no one was safe any longer. They began to lock their doors. Those who owned weapons made sure they were loaded. Those who had security alarms made sure they were working. Frankly, fear gripped the villagers that night. One could only wonder what the morning would bring.

Chapter 25

Cary threw the throttle into reverse and the boat slipped smoothly back into her berth. It amazed Calvin always how gently she handled his craft. He put out the bumpers; then secured the bow and stern lines as Cary shut off the engine. It was early, only 12:30pm; the afternoon was just beginning. Most boats returned between 4:00 and 5:00pm.

Tuna Ridge paid off big time this morning for Calvin two small makos, averaging between one hundred twenty pounds to one hundred fifty and four small tunas weighing up to four hundred pounds. He had completed his brother's chef's order and was pleased. Shit, he thought, those old folks in my brother's center eat real good. Can't get fresher fish than I provide and the money is damn nice. Nathan knows I'm padding the bill and he doesn't care. Well, I learned how to pad a bill from the master, Nathan Cain, himself! He's screwing the government left and right. What an eccentric, ungenerous, skinflint he is. I guess it's in the genes. I'm pretty frugal myself. Hey, his chef, Tom, is no better. He's a crook, too, and pilfers the pantries so he and his fat wife, Maureen, can eat like a king and queen. If the people in the place knew what was going on they'd beat it the hell out of there. As Cary walked down from the helm she was thinking about Cal's latest mood swing. She was pissed and her voice reflected her feelings when she said, "Cal, you're nastier than ever. Are you going through male menopause? Shit, Cal, you better lighten up and don't ever curse me down like that again or you can find your self a new mate and I mean it this time." Calvin lashed out, "Cary, I ordered you to turn port, not starboard. I almost lost my fish." "You said starboard, not port. I'm not going deaf, Cal. You've got too much on your mind lately, and, what I don't know. You're a great fishermen but you've become a miserable Captain and I am not going to put up with any more of your bullshit. You're still troubled about losing the damn tournament." Calvin looked down at the stern deck and relied quietly, "Please forgive me, Cary, it's been a few weeks since I lost and I still have nightmares over it. That was a lot of money to lose. You're also right; I did say port not starboard. I better lighten up. I don't want to lose a master mate like you, Cary." Calvin looked her in the eye and squeezing her arm said, "I'm sorry; I really re-gret cursing you down, it won't happen again. Shake hands on it?" "Sure, there you go, Cal, right back to normal, let's keep it that way, we make a good team, you know." "Cary, I sure do know that!"

"Now I've been thinking about those three people who've gone missing. It's best if you bunk on board with me until this thing blows over. In fact, I order you, Cary, stay on board with me. I'll keep you nice and safe. Damn, Cary, I can't let anything happen to you." "Cal, that's very sweet of you and I know that under that hard ass of yours there's a tender side to you but don't keep it boxed up, Cal, let it out. You'll be surprised how many good friends you could make." "Be my good friend, Cary, I don't need anyone else." "You know I am, Cal, and thanks for the offer but I'm carrying one of your pistols. I'll be safe. You watch out for your own ass; all alone on this boat. At least where I live we set up a block watch. Shit, I know how you snore. Anyone could walk right in on you." "Yeah, Cary, you're right. Guess I'm going to lock up and sleep with a gun under my pillow, too."

They usually didn't talk so long, thought Cary. Things seem different now. Maybe Cal will talk to me more and tell me how he feels and what he thinks, I hope.

Chapter 26

Calvin pulled up to the back of Nathan's Center, walked to the rear door, unlocked the door to the freezer room and took the yellow and red cart. As he unloaded the crates of fish and arranged them on the shelves he noticed a coffin sitting on top of a gurney. Bewildered and wondering what new scheme Nathan was hatching this time, knowing for sure that his brother's lust for money had to be behind it, he was sure that whatever this was all about, one day Nathan's thirst would prove to be the undoing of his gluttonous appetite.

Just as he finished and was checking all the neat piles of fish he had stacked, Tom, the chef came in. "Hi Calvin; today's catch?" "You bet, Tom ; can't get fish fresher than this. Boy, your old folks will be in fish paradise tonight! What'll you serve them, mako or tuna?" "Maureen and the kids are stopping by at dinner time; their favorite is tuna. And besides the old folks don't know the difference between mako and tuna and catfish," he laughed, holding on to his large belly as it jiggled from side to side. Calvin felt like slugging him right there on the spot and hanging him on one of those cold, sharp meat hooks. He thought, your fat wife and those obese kids of yours are going to be eating fat-free again tonight. What a bunch of chubby faced, paunchy, wide-ass free loaders. In a loud disgusted voice he said, "Hey, Tom, I hope your family leaves some food for the patients here; they need food, too, can't survive on your jelly and bologna sandwiches," "Hey, Calvin," Tom retorted, "they get good food here; they're ten to twenty pound overweight." "Yeah, Tom, catch you later," as he pushed the heavy freezer door open, walked through to the outer door and thought, if only I had a lock.

Calvin rode the elevator to the first floor and walked through the foyer to Nathan's oak paneled office. Nathan watched his brother's massive bulk move ever so gracefully as he walked into his office. Wow, he thought, fishing keeps Cal in great shape. Calvin handed Nathan the bill for the fish and told him as he always did, "The freshest fish in Montauk is down in your freezer, Nat." "Sure thing Cal," I'm looking forward to having some. Well, Cal, it's been two weeks since I've seen you; how's the fishing and how is Cary?" "Both are doing real fine. It's fast and furious out there, brother, not slow and dying like in here." Nathan laughed, "That's for sure, Cal. Mom and Dad taught me about the downside of this business but your business drops dead in a few months, so.........."Talk about dead; what do you make of those disappearances, Nat, anybody you know?" "Yes, Cal, I know Sabrina; she closed the deal on my new house awhile ago. It was her first sale. She made a pretty dollar on me. Yeah, this whole business is crazy, Cal, go figure. They just go missing. What do you think; UFO's circling Montauk or what?" They both had a hearty laugh. "Shit, beats me, Nat, I'm too busy fishing; have no time or interest in what's happening in Montauk."

Nathan walked over to his office door and locked it. Calvin knew that was the sign that Nathan wanted to talk business. "What's on your mind, Nat?" "Oh, just have a little something I want to discuss with you," Nat offered, as he sank into his leather desk chair. "Cal, how would you like to make some extra money, especially now with your off season approaching?" "Sure, Nat, as long as it's not illegal, I'm game." "I assure you Cal, it's not illegal but it fits smack damn into the gray area." "And, what's that suppose to mean, Nat; you don't get life just ten years with good behavior?" Nathan chortled smugly as he said, Now,

Cal, as you know, all businessmen including your self work in the gray zone. That, dear brother, is how we make our profit. The government is sucking the life out of us with every new tax they can come up with and they produce nothing, Cal, and they take our hard earned money." Nat purposefully proposed his next question, "Cal, do you think that's right?" "You know exactly how I feel about the government; what's your point?" "Exactly, Cal, that's how all businessmen feel, that's why we work in the gray zone. They fuck us and we fuck them. See, Cal, it's a perfect partnership, otherwise capitalism would soon disappear. Don't you agree, Cal?" "You're not talking to one of those idiots who you sweet talk into leaving their parents and shirking their responsibilities, Nat. I don't like talking in riddles; what did you scheme up this time?" "Okay, Calvin, now, we all recycle, right, Cal, and in this case I just want to recycle Mrs. Flannagan. She's rooming in the freezer as we speak." "What do you mean, you want to recycle her?" "Simply put, Cal, she's either going into the fire or the soil or the water. Now, that's where you come in. You fish the canyon, right, Cal, it's down hundred or so feet deep out there, right, so, Cal, just tie a fifty pound anchor to her and - voila - Mrs. Flannagan will be buried at sea."

"I've heard and seen a lot of weird shit but this tops them all, Cal. Are you out of your fuckin' mind?" "No, not at all, Cal, this is the perfect solution to my Flannagan dilemma. It's quick, it's clean, and, besides she always wanted to go fishing, Cal, now's her chance." "Now I know you're out of your fuckin' mind! Hey, Nat, were you involved in those three disappearances, too?" "Don't be ridiculous. This is just business, Cal, we'll both benefit. See the government money will be tax free. Now, we can get even with those dens of thieves."

Cal pondered for a long minute. "What's my cut?" "Aaaaah, that's my brother; tax free money always turns you on, right Cal? "Four hundred a month for the next two years, agreed?" "No way, Nathan, I'm taking the risk here, brother, and I know you get twelve hundred a month per resident. I'm running the risk of losing my Captain's license and boat and surer in hell prison time while you sit here in you oak, oval office; eight-four or no deal." "Okay, okay, Cal, but I, too, am taking a gamble, you know all the paper work leaves a paper trail right back to me." "If I know you, brother, Nathan, and I do know you, I'm surer in hell know it leads to a dead end." "Okay, six-six, Cal, and that's my best offer." "You can take your best offer and shove it, Nathan; seven-five or I'm walking right out of here."

Cal turned toward the door as Nathan swallowed hard and needed a drink of his trusty spring water. "Okay, Cal, you got me by the gills, 7-5 and it's a deal. You fishermen are tough bargainers." "No, Nathan, we're just trying to stay afloat." "How about some water Cal, one for the road?" Cal helped himself to a bottle, turned toward the door again and said, "By the way, Nat, what about Flannagan's relatives?" "That's the best part of the deal, Cal. She was ninety four; no family, no relatives. She simply outlived them all!" "You're a weasel Nathan; you'll burn in the fires of hell." "Brother, I'll see you down there, too." They both had a merry old laugh and shook hands.

"When Cal?" "Tomorrow morning Mrs. Flannagan and I have an appointment at the canyon. Nat, can't you get it for up to three years?" "Cal, trust me, that's pushing it. Don't want to bring attention to those fuckin' government auditors. Don't worry; I know how to milk it." "Okay, Nat, I'm out of here. Write my check, I need the money." Nathan opened his large check ledger, wrote the check quickly, handed it to Cal and informed him, "A Mrs. Di Palma is on the way out, same circumstances, brother, are you interested?" "Don't push, Nat, let's see how Mrs. Flannagan goes." "Okay, brother, Cal; you know how to let yourself out." "Yeah, see you Nat on my next delivery or my next pickup." "Have a good day, Cal." "You too, Nat."

Calvin pulled up to the center at 4:30am. He lowered Mrs. Flannagan into one of his medium six tuber tuna bags, sealed the Velcro and thought since this type of bag kept the tuna fresh Mrs. F. should do just fine. He placed the bag in the rear seat and concealed it with all sorts of fishing gear. As a final touch, he draped netting over her. Satisfied with his cunning deception and thinking how much the back seat looked like a typical fisherman's truck, he smiled devilishly. Didn't think I had it in me, he mused.

Once back on his boat, Calvin packed Mrs. F neatly in ice. She was now all set for her one way trip to the canyon. As he closed the freezer door, Cary startled him, shouting, "Good morning, Captain, top of the morning to you, sun is on the rise and I guess we should be heading out; long run today." "Good morning, Cary, glad to see you're early. I sure got the best mate in the entire fleet! Take her out. I'm going to catch a wink." Calvin never dreamed his task would have unnerved him but Cary's bright, cheery voice, earlier that usual did and a nap, he hoped, would calm him down. "Oh yeah, I know your winks, Cal, try to keep the sawing down or I'll have to blast the radio." "Sure thing, Cary; wake me when we get there."

As usual it was another long hard day of fishing but most rewarding having caught a mako, two tiger

179

sharks, three small tuna and a few mahi- mahi. Calvin reckoned it was a really fine day when he focused on his tax free seven hundred dollars that Nathan would be paying him each month. "I suppose I'll have to go 50-50 with him on Mrs. Di Palma," he said to himself, "but, why not, that's a net of thirteen hundred tax free government bucks. Fuck you, Uncle Sam, it's my turn to play robber."

Chapter 27

Elizabeth and Reese were having an intoxicating day surfing the ground swells as a result of the east south east currents that pushed amazing waves toward shore. They could not be luckier! The two were surfing the second cove on the ocean, west of Turtle Cove where the Lighthouse stood, known as the Pill Box or Rat Hole, The couple had the perfect wave pattern; a spacing of twelve seconds between each wave. It was ideal for surfing, and, of course, good exercise. The action was grand as they could cut left or right on their boards and maintain a consistent water speed of twenty miles an hour. The wind, blowing gently, at exactly ten miles per hour, off the shore line, swelled the waves, keeping them high, tight and crisp.

It was a glorious fall day. The bright sun illuminated great energy and the sky was filled with a palette of mixed azure colors. Eight nimbus clouds seemed to dance in the gentle breeze. This splendid afternoon for a ride offered the surfers a number of choices; long boards, big wave gun, potato chip, short thin board, fisher's short thin board and other smaller fun boards. Water temperature was sixty nine degrees: Elizabeth and Reese chose their two mil black wet suits. Elizabeth used her big wave gun and Reese his fisher's board. They had been surfing for three hours.

Sitting on his board and checking his watch which read 1:00pm, Reese knew it was lunchtime. Elizabeth's southern fried chicken was mouth watering. They decided to head in; last ride until after lunch. Food and a bit of rest would build up their energy for the rest of their day.

He wore his kaki shorts and matching shirt as most of the fishermen did during the warm September days. He thought the two figures on the ocean looked like two black phantoms, dancing and disappearing sharply into the curl of the waves. Riding closer to the beach they were balanced like two ballerinas ending their final pirouette for their midday set.

Elizabeth and Reese swung their hips and shifting their weight, forcing the boards to cut deeply into the water and came to a sudden stop. They jumped into the shallow water and took off their Velcro safety straps. Walking across the beach and up a small rocky incline, they leaned their boards against a large limb that some passing storm had brought to its final resting place. Together they set up a small beach table; took their goodies from the picnic basket and set everything on the little table. There was crispy southern fried chicken, potato and macaroni salad, a tossed salad, cole slaw, bottles of spring water and a cool bottle of Chablis with two wine glasses. "Let's eat, drink and relax, then re-wax our boards and hit the high waves again," Reese said. Bright eyed and taking her first bite of chicken, Elizabeth agreed. Reese thought no outsiders; that's damn rare under these beautiful conditions. Hell, I'm not calling anybody; half the down islanders would drive up here.

Their lunchtime music was provided by nature. As the waves came crashing to shore, all at once, like a symphony, the small rocks would be rolled up the shore line by the wave action rushing through them and resounding in a wonderful high pitched ringing sound. This was repeated as the waters receded pulling the stones downward. It was a never ending melodic tune as the rocks rolled dancingly back and forth. Depending upon the wave energy it ever so often changed the notes of the singing.

As they were enjoying their picnic, he appeared, holding his eight foot heavy duty fishing pole that he used for jetty and rock fishing. "Hi," he said and waved. "You guys are great. I was watching you from the bluffs." "Thanks," Reese managed to say, finishing a bite of chicken, "It looks easy but it took us many years of practice. We mastered it finally but there's always something new to learn. This is a fast sport; forever changing, you know, new waxes and boards." "Yeah, like fishing. Just when you think you have the best rod or reel or line they come out with something new. It keeps the economy moving and our pockets empty." They all laughed. He inquired, "Did you see any boils while you were out there?" They both looked puzzled. "Oh, I'm sorry, a fish boil happens when the bait is on top of the water and the bass or blues are pounding away at it. There is so much activity; the water going every which way as the bait tries to escape from the predators. We call it a boil." Good, he thought, they don't know anything about fishing. He knew this was the best time to make his move. It was dead low tide, no currents, therefore, no bait or fish. No self righteous fisherman would be caught down here at this time of day.

It was time to set his plan in motion however ironically it was prepared for him. He had planned to take care of both of them right there on the beach, but as luck would have it, Elizabeth, holding up the bottle of Chablis and smiling asked, "I know this is going to sound dumb but is it possible you would have a cork screw, we forgot ours?" "It happens all the time down here. I have one in my glove compartment. I'm parked right next to you." "Oh that's great; I'll walk back with you, uh what's your name?" "Sean O'Reilly, what's yours?" "Reese," shaking his hand, "and that's Elizabeth, my bride of eight months." "Elizabeth," Sean nodded, "Congratulations, welcome to Montauk, the End." They laughed. "Or it could be the beginning," added Elizabeth. "Sean would you like a piece of chicken, there's plenty, I always make enough to escape from that dreaded question, "what's for dinner"; we have enough for tonight." Sean thanked her, "First let's get the cork screw." "Elizabeth, we'll be right back, honey."

They walked to Sean's truck. Reese asked. "How's the fishing?" "Good Reese, good, had some nice size bass yesterday, right down by the Pill Box, hope they move in again tonight. The cork screw is in the glove compartment, Reese; keep it as a wedding present." "That's real nice of you. Is everybody in Montauk as friendly as you are?" "We're just a bunch of good old guys, Reese. After the tourists leave we get real laid back." Reese opened the truck door, bent slightly, and pushed the glove compartment button.

185

Like the grim reaper, he swung his pole like a sickle, full force, crushing the crown of Reese's somewhat balding head. The pressure of the blow slammed him up against the door and the front seat, wedging him in; holding him up. Good, he thought, taking the plastic bag out of his pocket and placing it over Reese's head. He pulled the rip cord tight, "let's keep it clean, Reese, you know, no evidence." He carried him over to the back of his truck, covered him under the canvas and hurried back along the path to Elizabeth.

He approached her from the right side. She never heard him or felt his presence, so intent was she holding up her drumstick, swinging it back and forth like a conductor's baton, playing to the rhythm of the rocks. He arched his pole and thrust it with such violent energy that upon contact the right side of her face crumpled half way into the left side. Her smashed face reminded him of a crushed car fender. He bagged her, jerked her up on his right shoulder and ripped the 'baton' she was clutching out of her hand. "Wow, that was delicious, just like Mom's," he said.

Suddenly, he heard them and could see that they were staring at him, watching every move he made. All six of them were potential witnesses. He did not panic. Instead, he stared right back at them. If I try for my truck, he thought, they'll make a move for it.

Think man, think. You have Elizabeth on you shoulder; they see her, too. They're probably thinking I can't make it back to my truck with all this additional weight. Screw them, I'll show those bastards who's in command around here. Quick, he thought, take charge of the situation. They seem to be waiting for me to make the first move. He wondered if they had seen him as he killed both of them. All of a sudden, in one fell swoop, he bent down and snatched the entire tray of southern fried chicken. Looking up, he saw them. The seagulls were circling and staring at the tray. They sure reminded him of those feather brained politicians who were always looking for a handout. He wished he could snap their scrawny necks.

He hid Elizabeth next to Reese, placing her left arm around his shoulder, thinking, you guys were really dancing out there. He covered them, grabbed the chicken and took off. He knew it would be impossible to discover the tire track on this hard, rocky road. As he gazed toward the beach, he caught sight of those free loaders, diving for the remains of the picnic.

Chapter 28

The sky was an incandescent blue over the Police Department Headquarters Building. It was another beautiful day weather-wise, unlike the somber atmosphere in the Control Center where Todd and Roy were discussing the recent events. Today was the third day since Sabrina had vanished.

Roy was busy reading several reports completed by the various teams working the cases while Todd was adding new information, theories, guesswork and hunches to his charts. Roy, discouraged, glanced up from his pile of investigative communications that all added up to zero and said glumly, "Todd, nothing. That ferryman of yours must be the devil; he just appears and disappears as he pleases, not leaving a clue. It's mind boggling, Todd, down right mind boggling." "Police work is not easy, Roy, every scrap of evidence has to be analyzed, all leads have to be followed and there are all those interviews that have to be conducted......." Roy, interrupted, "shit, we don't even have a crime scene. Then there's all that dull, tedious paper work and records which have to be gone through. The investigating teams are coming up empty handed. What the hell are we missing? No bodies, foul play ruled out. No blood or any evidence that a crime has been committed; not a witness or phone tip. We have your theories, Todd, but are they workable?" "You're right about evidence, buddy, but they didn't disappear willingly, Roy."

"Okay, Todd, here's my ferryman check list to date: X means nothing, get it? 1. dog team-X 2. nature lover's interviews-X 3. interviews with close relatives, families, friends, ex-boyfriend or girl friend-X 4. credit cards-X 5. email-X 6. residence searches-X 7. bank accounts-X 8, home telephone records-X 9. cell phones records-X 10. FBI-missing person data base-X 11. victims' scene-X 12. evidence and clues-X 13. fingerprints-X 14. forensics-X 15, Retired Captain North telephone company connection-X. Nothing, Todd, I keep coming up with more questions for which I have no answers. We shot all those photos we pinned up on that wall over there." Pointing to them, Roy, continued, "nice house in this one, there's a clean blue SUV over here, nice trees and grass in this one and look at that pile of rocks under the Lighthouse." Todd felt Roy's dejection and frustration and trying to lift his spirits he walked over to him, put his hand on his shoulder, "Okay, Sergeant, the case may appear to be weary, flat, clueless, stale and unproductive but trust me, Roy, the FERRYMAN is going down. Trust my hunches, Roy, my instincts, my beliefs and my intuition. The bastard will be subdued. He's not infallible; he'll make a mistake and that's when we'll checkmate him." Todd cleared his unusually dry throat, "My old John Jay college professor kept pounding this into my head, 'he may baffle you at first, there will definitely be setbacks but you most certainly will triumph over evil.'"

Early Friday morning Todd and Roy were still as it in their Control Center when the red phone rang. They both turned and just stared as they listened to the several rings. When Todd picked up finally, his face said it all. "Roy, another possible disappearance, let's move."

Todd was not comfortable speeding at 85 miles per hour with the lights flashing and the siren blaring especially since he was not behind the wheel. "Roy, why in hell are we traveling so damn fast to a scene that State Park Sergeant Steve Lubell has already secured?" "I don't know, Todd, it's always done like this, you know, like in the Army, hurry up and wait," he chuckled. "Roy, slow down," Todd ordered, "to fifty five. I have a family I want to see again and besides this is an area crawling with deer. I sure in hell don't we one crashing through the windshield, landing on my lap." Roy laughed, "Oh, shit, Todd, don't take the little bit of fun we have once in awhile on the job. I'm well trained as a driver by the academy." "Yeah, Roy, did they also inform you that hitting a deer at eighty five would be like smashing into a stone wall?" Roy looked at Todd, winked and lightened up on the gas pedal. "You're right, why the hell, are we rushing anyway, there's going to be no clues, leads and absolutely no ferryman, just another disappearance. It's all hopeless, Todd, just another wild goose chase." "Do you recall, Roy, what my professor told me?" 'Yeah, yeah, baffles, setbacks, good over evil; all the words are cool, Todd, but this guy doesn't make mistakes." "He will, Roy, trust me, he will." Roy perked up and pushed the pedal a little harder.

When they arrived at the scene they saw that Sergeant Lubell had already yellow taped the surrounding picnic area. "I wish we could meet under better circumstances," Lubell said dismally, pointing to the picnic area. "Look at the disarray; plastic containers every which way, wine bottle next to the broken glasses, some water bottles broken; some still in tact and oddly enough one chicken bone in the basket. My guess is that it's a drumstick. I should know, chicken's my favorite, must have eaten a million of them. Anyway, shit, it had to be the seagulls that messed up this area. See those gray and white feathers in the picnic basket and around the broken glass? No doubt about it, Todd, you leave food around unguarded and those beggars are on it like flies on horseshit."

Todd was thinking speculatively, why just one chicken bone? It's obvious there were two of them, two glasses, two white forks, spoon and knives, two surf boards. "Sergeant Lubell, did you run the plate?" "Yep, belongs to R. Hawkins, 219 Arbor Lane, Middle Island, age twenty six, born 7/14/81. I sent two of my people over to his house. The sister was there, an Elaine Saris, sister to Elizabeth Hawkins, who informed my guys that Reese and Elizabeth took a day trip out here, left early Thursday morning to go surfing. She being from California just got in Wednesday night, said it was too early for her to go with them. I inspected their boards; both have their names on them."

Lubell glanced down at his notepad, "the sister said they had a picnic basket filled with a large tray of southern fried chicken, wine, water and various salads. That's it, Todd, nothing further." "Sergeant, you said a tray of chicken, how may pieces and what kind?" "Hold on, Todd, I'll get you the information." "Todd," asked Roy, "what are you thinking; we got something?" "Bingo, Roy, you'll make a detective yet. Think about it, just one bone, probably a drumstick, agreed?" "Agreed," replied Roy. "Ask yourself, Roy, why only one bone when they had a whole chicken? Where the hell are the other bones?" After a pause, Todd said, "Seagulls can't swallow large chicken bones; they would get caught in their throats and good bye seagull. So, Roy as Sherlock Holmes would have asked Watson, 'where are the bones'? And, Roy, why is that one there in the picnic basket?" Roy blinked and shrugged his shoulders, "aaaaah, someone took them?" "There you go, Roy, just let it out." "Uh, probably fishermen or raccoons." "No, Roy, HE TOOK THEM. I suspect he sampled that drumstick and with any luck we'll have a print. Call forensics; get them up here fast before this scene gets any dirtier." "Yes sir," answered Roy, feeling his pulse picking up speed.

"Todd," asked Sergeant Lubell, "she said there was an assortment of twenty five pieces; Reese and Elizabeth love their fried chicken, so what I want to know is where the hell, are the rest of the bones? I never saw a seagull eat chicken bones. I know everybody loves fried chicken but...""Right," remarked Todd," so does he." "Holy shit, what kind of a nut job are we dealing with, Lieutenant?" "Good question, Sergeant."

The three officers stared down into the basket at the one bone. "If luck will have it we may have his prints, boys," Todd said again. As they stood there they could hear the wailing siren from the forensic team approaching. "It will be their show now," Todd told the others, adding, "a bastardly scene, created by a madman." Better get back to Headquarters, Todd felt and inform the Chief. "Let's move, Roy." They waved to Sergeant Lubell and took off.

On the way back Todd and Roy stopped at Jack's to up date him and the guys on the latest disappearances. It wasn't long before practically the whole village was talking about the double vanishings.

Chapter 29

When Todd left the Chief's office after their conference, he returned to the Control Center with a feeling of emptiness in his belly; he knew he needed food but more important; the ferryman. "Let's break for lunch, Roy." "Fine with me, Todd, I'm hungry, where we off to?" "Jack's, of course, he make a tasty fish and chips."

As they walked through the door at Jack's the door bells jingled their usual tune, signaling to Jack more customers. Jack, refilling his coffee pot, turned his head around, spied Todd and Roy coming in and excitedly said, "Over here, guys, I'll clean off this table in a wink."

The corner table was a strategic spot for Jack to get enough gossip for the night. "Todd the usual?" "Sure, Jack." "Roy?" "Same for me, Jack" "Okay, that's two fish and chips in the basket with cold slaw, any coffee?" Both nodded. "Coming right up and believe me the flounder is the best in town; just caught locally." "Thanks, Jack," Todd said, biting on a new green pickle. Jack asked anxiously, "Anymore to tell me since you've seen the Chief?" "No, Jack, you'll be the first to know after us. You're part of the team and I depend upon you to keep me informed if you hear anything from the guys that might shed some light, any light, on these cases. You're my control Center Number Two." Jack was almost bowled over, thinking, I'm a member of the investigative team; my coffee house is Center Two! "Okay, guys," he said, trying to compose himself to the wonder of it all. I'll be right back," as he yelled to Fred, "two big baskets." "Great," exclaimed, Todd, "he's giving us extra fish and fries, Roy. Jack knows how to keep his off season customers coming back. He's a shrewd businessman alright, that pot of coffee he carries around is his fishing lure; Jack has half the town hooked."

While they waited for their order, Todd received a call from Detective Sergeant Jim Menthe. "We have what appears to be a good thumb print, Todd. You were right, it's a drumstick. He might have held it by his thumb inside his palm. We did ultra light on it; it's a perfect thumb print and as we talk, Todd, it's on the way to FBI Finger Print Data Base Division. They guarantee twenty four hour turn around to my office. Damn good work, Todd, this might just break the case." Smiling at Roy, Todd announced "We have a thumb print!" Roy dropped his pickle on the table. "What the hell you say, a thumb print?" Todd put his fingers to his mouth. Roy clammed up. Jack who overheard the chatter, thought, thumb print, we may have broken this case in my coffee house, as he visualized the crowd lines outside. "Anything, else detective?" Todd asked, "No, Todd, we used the dog teams, searched the area; nothing, no tire tracks, no other prints other than those of the victims all over everything. Hopefully, by tomorrow, we'll have that bastard." "Thanks, Jim; get back to me as soon as you get anything." "Roger that Todd."

Roy was on the fast track, "We have him Todd?" "No, forensics picked up one thumb print, FBI will run it through their data base," explained Todd. "You and your professor were right; just persevere 'til he slips up. Now we have a print and that signifies progress, Todd." "Don't get your hopes up, buddy, it's one thumb print to be matched against millions of others; the probability of coming up with a suspect is a billion to one, but, Roy, there's another possibility. Remember, Roy, he hasn't given up a legitimate clue or left evidence. Why, Roy?" Roy's face looked troubled as he answered, "You think he's toying with us, trying to throw us off? We have a print and with today's technology and FBI's advance electronics they should be able to come up with something, right?" "It doesn't work that way, Roy, you need three to five prints to do a true cross checks against their enormous data base volumes." "Let me get this straight, Todd, if this is his print or it's not his print we're still at a dead end?" "Not quite, Roy, this is hard nose police work.

"This enigma, we are investigating", explained Todd, is not inexplicable at this time; it's a matter of finding answers, discovering some clues or evidence with which to work thereby turning up solutions to the questions; as they say, 'cracking the case.' Simply put, buddy it's trial and error and we just have to keep at it. He's not infallible. We may have received our first break; the law of averages is turning in our favor. It's all up to the clocksettter." "The clocksetter?" "Father Time, Roy, I'm beginning to get on to him; in fact I'm getting a better feel for him. He's not unlike you or me, Roy, he could be sitting right here in Jack's enjoying lunch." Roy squinted and scanned all the faces in the coffee shop.

Jack showed up with their lunches, sat down, and placed his coffee pot on the table. He whispered, "So, Todd, we have a finger print, ah, I mean a thumb print?" "Yes, Jack let's hope that coffee pot of yours helps to turn the tide for us. We need a break, Jack, we need it bad. We're up to five disappearances."

Back at Headquarters, Todd filled the Chief in on the thumb print. The Chief didn't hold out much hope after dealing with the FBI in the past but he did praise Todd for his clever work of finding the print on the drumstick.

Todd returned to his lair and added Reese's and Elizabeth's names to his profile chart, their SUV information, their status before vanishing; surfing, picnic basket and contents. Under the column titled evidence he wrote thumb print in red letters. He stood back and looked for any similarities between all the missing people. There appeared to be none, but, that, too proved to be something. He felt these were random disappearances; however, all were intentional and premeditated. He walked over to the Ferryman chart and wrote, also in red, possible thumb print; awaiting FBI results.

It was late; another long day, Roy had already left. Todd grabbed his jacket and wondered what tomorrow would bring.

Chapter 30

It was early Saturday morning, the sun on the rise, as Cary went to the helm and found Calvin reading his engine manual. "What's with the manual, Cal?" "Happy Birthday, Cary." "Oh, yes, thank you, Cal." "We're not fishing today, Cary, have to change the water pump. It gave up the ghost, so to speak." "Talk about giving up the ghost, Cal, did you hear that two more went missing; a husband and a wife? They were surfing up at Pill Box." "Really, I didn't hear a thing, you're the only one that's social, I don't even listen to the radio or TV for that matter. You know me, Cary. But that's a damn shame, especially a man and wife. I've always said you got to be prepared. Right my mate?" "How the hell do you prepare for not vanishing Cal?" "Simply stay home until they catch this nut." "What do you think he's doing with the bodies, Cal?" "How the hell would I know, Cary? I'm just trying to figure out how to replace this pump. It's in a tight area; there must be a trick to pulling her out."

"The town's all talk about the goings on; the newspaper people running all over the village. It's insanity, Cal! They're like vultures on a carcass. If you dare say I saw or knew that person, you'll have twenty cameras and mikes in your face before you can blink. They're documenting every inch of the beach from the village to the Lighthouse." "Cary, stay away from those people; they are half wits; men of straw; puppets of the networks." "Men of straw; now, where did you hear that one?" "It's just an old expression from Norway. Talking about dummies, Cary, I apologize for not picking up a birthday present for you. Here, take this, Cary, and go buy yourself a trinket, a fun thing like magical or something."

Cary put the one hundred bill in her pocket and wiped a tear with the back of her hand, thinking, how generous of her Captain. "Thanks, Cal, what a good idea! I know just the place to go. There's an old store down at the docks called, "Aladin's Lamp", giving Cal a peck on his cheekbone. "Cal, give me a call if we're going out tomorrow and thanks again for my birthday money!"

Cary drove directly to the magic shop. The sign on a white post outside the door read, "Aladin's Magic & Spiritual Needs" and underneath, in smaller print, "Tarot Card Readings". Cary walked to the front window and peeked through the glass. The dark shop seemed to flicker in candlelight. Oh well, she thought, it's a magic shop, so it should look a little spooky.

As she entered the shop a strong scent of jasmine spice curled up her nostrils. A queer feeling crept within her, as if, she thought, I've left the present and this must be the boundless past world of Houdini with all those strange magical time honored deceptions of illusion. Her eyes adjusted slowly to the low, fluttering, burning candle flames that shimmered and danced waveringly around the shop's odd and unique articles. Her eyes darted from one unusual novelty to the next. The perfumed tincture of jasmine, ever present, made her almost lightheaded.

"See anything that perks your interest, Cary?" Her voice was feminine and sweet, like that of an older, wiser woman. This voice that broke the silence seemed to echo throughout the shop, Cary thought, yet it startled her and when she turned and caught sight of an older woman, dressed all in black, she shivered. As the woman walked closer to her, Cary noticed a gold chain around her neck which evidently held something but was hidden beneath the woman's black sweater. Her dark hair was thick with silvery gray steaks and reached down to the middle of her back. Those dark eyes reflected the flickering candlelight. Her facial expression was invitingly warm, actually enchanting to Cary. The woman was thin and slightly bent forward and her white cane contrasted her dark appearance.

"Hello," Cary managed to say. "How did you know my name?" "My name is Simone, Cary. I read tarot cards. They told me I would have a special guest in my shop today. I'm also clairvoyant at times and this gift tells me things; like your name just popped into my head. It runs in the family. My great grandmother could foretell the future but over the generations the gift has waned."

Simone sat down on a small green velvet wing back chair and motioned Cary to sit next to her on a charming, white wicker club chair. Simone began graciously to identify the various items she had in her small, crowded eclectic shop.

Cary was fascinated as Simone pointed to the good luck charms and the love charms hanging from the branch of a four foot tree which was set on one of the counter tops. A display of unique jewelry including magic rings and necklaces to keep the evil eye away glittered on black felt. Shelves were filled with all sorts of magic tricks and illusions. On one table there were spirit wheels, candles, sacred bells and incense. Tarot books and cards, ouija boards, an assortment of astrology books and ritualistic manuals were spread out like a fan on a long wooden table. There were all sorts of herbs and potpourri in clay bowls. Beautiful, feathery dream catchers hung from delicate gold ribbons.

Cary felt as if she was in another world. "What a bewitching, mystical and intoxicating room I am in," she said to Simone. "But you are not here for these items, are you, Cary?" Cary just stared deeply into Simone's flickering eyes and felt drawn by the power they possessed. "Cary, don't be fearful, my grandmother was able to call the spirits from the vast deep. I feel the great world of flight that lies behind all human destinies and I assure you, Cary, I doubly assure you there is a peace and harmony within your light. You're a just and kind person. However, there is an evil storm brewing among our lives; it's the autumn of our discontent. The divinity that stirs within you has reached out to me, I know what you seek, Cary. I know the purpose of your visit."

Cary was mystified but watched in anticipation as Simone got up, went behind the counter and held up a golden box. "Do you believe in legends, Cary?" "I believe in superstitions if that's what you mean." "That will do, Cary. What I am about to tell you is true. Simone returned to her chair, settled her cane on an arm, folded her hands in her lap and quietly cleared her throat. Cary, her back as straight as a ram rod, looked directly into Simone's hypnotic eyes.

Simone began, "Three generations ago in Hawaii a family went to the beach one, hot, steamy day. The husband fell asleep. His wife and two year old daughter went into the water to refresh themselves. They got caught in a rip and were pulled out off the reef. The husband awakened to the sounds of his wife screaming. He ran to the edge of the water. He felt helpless as he could not swim. Suddenly, he spotted a large dorsal fin rising out of the water. He watched as it moved directly toward his wife and his child. All at once its huge body pulled up along side of the mother and her child blocking their forward motion. As the mammoth black orca slowly eased them back to the beach, he stranded himself too close to the beach on the reef. The wife and daughter reached safety and on to the arms of the husband and father. No matter how hard the fish tried he could not escape his predicament. After awhile it just sat there basking in the sun. Its skin lost its moisture and hardened like leather. The whole little village came after hearing the story and everyone tried every measure they knew but to no avail.

The next morning the dear dead orca was lying on the sandy beach after the high tides carried him to shore. The villagers stripped every body part as a keepsake to ward off evil spirits. My great grandmother had five teeth from that orca."

Simone reached inside her sweater and pulled up a large white pointed tooth encased in gold. "This is one of them, Cary." Mesmerized, Cary stared wide eyed at the tooth, as Simone swung it back and forth in the dancing candlelight. Slipping her tooth back under her sweater and in a whispery voice said, "My two sisters and brother wear the other three."

Cary felt an unpleasant taste of nausea as the tooth vanished. What is happening to me, she wondered? Simone, sensing Cary's distress, picked up the golden box in her left hand, opened it toward her, hovered over its contents for a moment while Cary stared transfixed. Quickly, Simone's fingers swooped like a bird of prey into the box and pulled out the identical tooth to the one she was wearing. She held it high with one hand and used the other to grasp the chain allowing the tooth to dangle and shimmer in the candlelit shop.

"This was my mother's Cary, her mother passed it on to her. My grandmother was the woman in the water who was saved by the orca and the two year old child was my mother." Cary stiffened in astonishment. "Your mother was the child and her mother was your grandmother?" "Yes, Cary," Simone replied as she closed her dark eyes, "Yes, Cary, you are the special person my mother revealed to me this morning. You are now the safe-keeper of her tooth. She chose you to wear her tooth in these times of trouble; you're the sentinel of her dear orca's tooth. Cary, it will shield you from the wickedness that lurks out there."

No longer could Cary suppress her desire to hold the tooth. She moved closer. Stroking the tooth's smooth enamel surface seemed to exude even a more exquisite aura. "This gift is from my mother Cary and only upon your approaching death may you relinquish it to a new, just and deserving person. Have faith, my dear, it will guide you to its new keeper." Simone placed the chain carefully around Cary's neck as Cary clasped the tooth gratefully in her palm and whispered passionately, "until death do us part."

The stunning, amazing event overwhelmed Cary and all she could bring herself to say to Simone was, "thank you so very much. I feel humbled that your mother selected me." Simone put both her palms on Cary's warm, wet cheeks as she said, "Cary, I sense you will have a long and healthy life," and leaning forward, giving Cary the kiss of peace on her forehead, "go, my child, you have entered into the mystery of the cycle of light; it's now completed."

Bowing her head, Cary walked solemnly out of the curious, little shop, a sadder but wiser woman, as the salty sea air replaced the scent of jasmine in her nostrils. She might have stayed a little longer but somehow she knew her destiny was elsewhere. What she didn't know was that Simone knew emphatically where Cary's fate would take her.

Chapter 31

Thursday morning's sky was a mixture of cobalt blue with small white clouds that looked like the ocean breakers sweeping along their never ending voyage out to sea. It did not reflect the feelings of the villagers in this disturbed community.

Eight days had passed since Reese and Elizabeth had disappeared. Detective Jim Menthe was good to his word and called Todd within the twenty four hour period it took the FBI to run the print. It came up a no hit as Todd expected. Sitting at his desk, contemplating the data, Todd found only one apparent similarity; they had all disappeared without a trace. That was crystal clear but where did they go missing? Why did they go missing? What was the modus operandi behind the vanishings? These ominous questions baffled Todd and kept him awake at night. What am I missing? Why does he want them? Where does he keep them? How does he keep them? How does he ferry them in and out or does he? If they are kept here does he store them? How would he preserve them?

Gnawing questions and unthinkable ideas jammed Todd's mind. It seemed to him that the odious ferryman conducted his life without emotion, morals or ethics. There is a complete absence of virtues and he most certainly personifies the scarlet sin of evil. If he is an evil, born unto itself, Todd deduced, then what pains his mind to cause such horror? It seems his sincerest form of evil takes unprejudiced human life. He is a "sober" brute but has an inescapable face no one notices. Maybe, he's decided to bring Judgment Day upon us. In that case, he could be one of those religious homicidal nuts or looking to be the 'Prince of Terror'. Perhaps, he's after the crown of death; to be the best of the best. On the other hand, he might be telling us a psychopathic story or giving lessons in contradictions; dishing out slaughter and walking among us unseen. He strikes with a cunning brilliance he deems perfection. I dare to think of how many others will disappear before I get him. This monster is going to slip up and when he does I'll be waiting. The media is confounded by him, the villagers are tormented but I know the luck he covets will run out. There's a chance the task force may come up with something from the early morning searches. All long shots have to be played. We must make an impact on that ruthless killer and thankfully there has been a noticeable lapse of time since the last vanishing due to the fact that the 24-7 of the East Hampton Police, the State Park Police and the inquiries appears to have kept him out of action. We are the pursuers devoted to nailing his ass. He's not going to hornswaggle us forever.

Roy, in double time, came barging into the office, cutting off Todd's rambling, puzzling thoughts. He looked a "frothy frustration", thought Todd. "Roy, lighten up, you're starting to develop an attitude problem which we don't need around here. You're a Sergeant, act like one, otherwise it could become infectious. What we don't want is a bunch of fellow officers walking around long faced; that's not the image this department wants to project to the public, Roy." "Okay, okay, you're right. It's just so damn depressing and frustrating. I hate to use those words but nothing seems to describe my feelings - nothing. We're investigating every which way, getting no where. One of your theories about cold storage for the bodies we're looking for didn't pan out, Todd. The store owners, the bar tenders, and you name it, were cooperative with our searching. But, shit, the butcher made us take off our shoes. Can you imagine that?"

He handed Todd a long list. "We inspected every cold freezer in Montauk, as per your theory, including a big walk in at the Nursing Center. All checked out and were clean. Oh, the owner guy, a one Nathan Cain, was definitely pissed off that we were there; you would think he was implicated or something." "Roy, I hope you weren't too heavy handed with him; he's a respectable community businessman who carries a lot of influence around the town. I don't want the Chief's phone ringing off the hook."

"I think he must have taken them out of the village, Todd. This shit is creepy. Every freezer I opened I had expectations of seeing corpses. I'm a police officer for sure and carry side arms but even I'm getting a little spooked. You know, finger prints, dead ends, freezer nothings, no leads; shit who is this ferryman?" "Who is the million dollar question, Roy? You've got to remember, Roy, he's not infallible. He made one small slip, for sure, now he's due for a major one." "Yeah, Todd, that's what you keep telling me but he hasn't screwed up yet, especially after five disappearances. Hey, this is a little village so where in hell is he living?" "That's another good question. Now we have to change gears to find his rat's nest. By the way, Roy, did you check out my wine frig? "Why the hell would I do that? You're the team leader." "Roy, no one is above suspicion plus the villagers would be more open to our searches if they thought we were looking at ourselves, too. This is a mess, Roy, but I am determined to put the saddle on the right horse." "Okay, I'll inspect it first thing in the morning, Todd." "Don't' bother, I have to go to the store and make out the wine order. I'll check the frig with Gary and Clive. Okay, buddy, I'm through here for today. Catch you tomorrow."

Chapter 32

Todd parked in his familiar spot behind the liquor store. As he entered through the rear door he saw Clive and Gary studying their next chess moves. After the usual tasks were completed they often passed their days by playing chess between customers. "Hi guys," Todd greeted them and felt that a burden was lifted from his shoulders as once again he assumed his role of liquor store owner.

"Boy, it's good to be back, I missed this." Both friends looked up from the board pleased to see their boss and good friend. Todd glanced at their game. "Mate in four moves, Gary." Gary and Clive glared down at the board. Slightly agitated, Gary answered, "No way, Todd, I've got his ass on the run." Clive laughed, "Gary, I was seeing check mate in three moves but Todd is right. It's even better in four." Gary's eyes flashed from piece to piece desperately trying to discover the mating trap; he never saw it coming. Clive moved his bishop to queen knight five and in a victorious voice proclaimed check and shared a wink with Todd. Gary examined the men once again. His king was in check by the bishop one as that was the only move he had left. Clive pressed on king knight six check. Again Gary's king was in check, this time by the knight. Then Gary saw the check mate coming in two more moves and succumbed to Clive's overwhelming chess strategy by lowering his king down on the board which signaled his defeat. "That was some great move, Clive, you're a good tactician; seven games for you, two for me."

The front door opened wide as Cary walked in. Gary was just about to get up but Todd held up his hand to stop him. "I'll take care of Cary; she's my first customer in eight days!" Grinning, he said, "Good afternoon, Cary, my love, how's my favorite person in Montauk doing on this bluebird of a day?" "Oh, Todd, you really should go into politics; you speak such beautiful bullshit." Laughing, she went on, "but an old salt like me needs to hear those sweet words as I pass into time." "Cary, you remind me of a good bottle of wine; the longer you age, the better she tastes." "Oh, there you go, Todd, sure in hell you have a gifted and blessed tongue. You're good, Todd. Is that how you won over Jamie?" "Well, pretty much, I guess, Cary, but she could see through the bullshit, too." "You know, lad, I'm just Calvin's mate hoping for a possible merger one of these fine days." All three cheered and whistled.

"Speaking of Calvin, Cary, how's he doing?" "Ah, after the loss of the tournament, he's like a mako on the end of the line. "You can't blame him Cary; that was a lot of money you both lost," Clive said sadly as Todd and Gary agreed. "Yes, guys, you're right, but he did sweeten my palm with a one hundred dollar bill the other day for my birthday!" In unison all three said quickly, "Happy Birthday, dear Cary."

Smiling her lovely wide smile, "Oh thank you, fellas, you guys are so dear. Anyway, off I went to that quaint little magic shop, you know, Alladin's Lamp; it's full of magical things. Look here," as she pulled out the orca's tooth from under her parker. It glittered in the sunlight shining in from the large store front window.

The three stared fascinated by its brilliance. After a few moments, Todd commented, "That's extraordinary, Cary," examining it thoughtfully, "you found this in that shop?" Cary was indeed thrilled to have the opportunity to tell them all about the mystical legend of her precious gift from Simone. "I can almost feel the tooth's powers tugging at me, Cary," Todd exclaimed after hearing the story. "I wish we had one for every person in Montauk, Todd. Are you getting any closer to this ferryman?" "How the hell did you know I dubbed him the ferryman, Cary?" "The whole village is talking of him as the ferryman, you know, 'sotto voce' rules Montauk, Todd." "Yes Cary, 'sotto voce' may rule Montauk but I'm going to rule a certain Sergeant first thing tomorrow." "No, Todd, leave poor Roy alone, you know he's family; we're all in this together. Todd, please don't go picking on Roy, for all I know it could have been the Chief's wife."

"What do you mean, 'the Chief's wife'?" Todd asked incredulously. "Well, Jack and Lily have that rare gift of gab, you know, they sit in at corner table up front by the kitchen and Jack keeps filling her coffee cup while she chatters away, and Jack, playing the part of the good natured bartender, pumps Lily 'til he gets his fill of all that rich gossip he needs for his day. Then after she leaves Jack becomes the spokesman of his coffee house. Don't you know he loves it?" "Damn it Cary, how did you know about this?" "Simple, Cal and I get back early from fishing lately and one of my chores is to pick up his dinner. Believe me Todd, it's a daily happening." "So Cary, once Jack gets an earful, all Montauk is ablaze with the fire of that chatter and the gossips put two and two together and get five. Is that what you're telling me?" "Any choice bit of dirt goes along way in this hamlet, Todd," Cary replied confidently.

Clive spoke up, "Todd we heard the thumb print was a no hit." "Todd stared at Clive with the eyes of a falcon. "Who did you hear that from Clive?" "I truly don't remember but it was at Jack's." Todd didn't reply but thought to himself that the leaks had to end or the investigation would be hindered badly or perhaps, on the other hand, the situation could be advantageous. If false data was leaked and spread throughout the village it might confuse the ferryman and lead to his mistakes.

Cary, holding her tooth up to Todd, said knowingly, "Todd this tooth is the evil chaser." "I really wish Cary it was the evil chaser." "Todd, you know, down in New Orleans if you cut the King Cake and find the baby; it's good luck for all year. But now that I have the dear orca's tooth I'm set for life." "That's great Cary, so now, what'll be, light rum or dark rum?" "I think I'll go for dark today." "Okay, my love, dark it shall be." He gift wrapped the rum as Cary watched and said "What's with the fancy paper?" Todd handed her the gift wrapped bottle, "Happy Never Too Late Birthday Cary and many, many more! Give Calvin my regards. We don't see enough of him anymore. I know he like his Wild Turkey down at Salador's but he could pay us a visit once in awhile." "No way Todd; Cal likes his ship mates down there. He feels comfortable with them, you know, all that quid pro quo shit; that just they understand. It's all part of the fishing brother-hood out here." "Right Cary, thanks for coming love. See you soon. God Bless, Cary."

Todd sat down to begin to write the wine order but first did a quick calculation of the past two week's business. Surprised to learn that his sales had doubled made him only more aware of the fact that the villag-ers were definitely afraid. Unfortunately or fortunately he figured that this missing persons' predicament had increased monetary benefits for the restaurants and bars since they offered congenial companionship to those who needed to be with others. He knew Jack's was packed tighter than a can of tuna fish.

Gary and Clive completed checking the wine frig and reported to Todd that there were only wine bot-tles, no bodies. Todd thanked his friends and assured them he would tell Roy he was clean.

Chapter 33

He was up at dawn's first light. Shortly after, he headed for the docks to have his usual breakfast at Salador's. He caught sight of her coming out of the fog. Her thumb was begging for a ride. He pulled off the road ahead of her and reaching over unlocked the door. She opened it, saying, "Hi, I'm Carolina; need a ride to the Montauk Train Station." "I'm Sean," and shook her small, cool hand. Settling herself in, as he watched, he said, "This early morning fog is getting thick like pea soup. It's coming off the bays with the southwest winds. So where you off to, Carolina, so early this morning, going shopping in the big city?" "Not really," she answered. "I'm just getting the hell out of here, change of life, you might say." "So you're running away? What, your parents don't give you enough allowance or they are too damn tough on you?" "Yeah, and all that shit I have to put up with. I'm sixteen and

they treat me like I'm an outcast. I can never do anything right in their eyes so I decided to move in with
my older sister who lives in the city." "Oh, really, just
like that, up and out, cast responsibilities to the wind?
What about your schooling?" "I'll go to one of those
city schools; my sister did it on her own, if she can so
can I." "What about your parents and how are they
going to feel after you're gone? "Frankly, I don't give
a damn. They treat me like shit anyway." "I see your
point, Carolina. Then it's off to the train station, my
lass"

He reached under the driver's seat, grabbing his
round club and swinging it in an upward motion
smashed her young smart assed sixteen year old forehead in half. She had just put a cigarette in her mouth
and while fidgeting for her lighter in her purse never
saw it coming. He slammed her head into the back
of the seat, replaced the club under his seat, whipped
out a plastic bag, placed it over her head and pulled
tightly on the rip cord. He shoved her down into the
forward compartment, covered her with a green and
yellow plaid blanket, put the truck into drive, made a
u- turn and headed back to his asylum.

Early in the morning on the first day of October,
the birds and deer were foraging actively for food in
the back yard of the Roget's five acre home, located

along the lake. Mark and Fern Roget, avid nature lovers extraordinaire, carried any cause to do with the environment to an extreme degree. They were stiff, arrogant social climbers whose personal interests were devoted to status. They named their two daughters after two liberal environmentally-minded states. California nineteen years old left home at age seventeen and found solace in Greenwich Village. Her sister, Carolina, age sixteen, just about tolerated her parents and had decided it was time to join her sister in New York City.

The telephone rang five times before Mark Roget even attempted to answer it since he was engrossed in one of his many "natural world" dry, exaggerated and half-truths books. Finally, letting out a long sigh and rolling his eyes, he lifted the receiver, "Mr. Mark Roget here," he announced in his uppity voice. "Mr. Roget, this is Mr. Durkin," said the principal of the local high school. "Your daughter, Carolina, did not show up for her first class today. Is she sick?" "Hell, if I know; hold on, I'll get my wife," he replied indifferently.

Fern Roget picked up the cordless phone. "Mr. Durkin, I checked her room; it's tidy as ever, she's not here. I'm sure she's just late." "Probably so," agreed the principal, "she did tell some of her friends she was having a party last night since yesterday was her birthday."

"Her birthday, a party, ah uh, oh, oh yes, we had a party for her," stuttered Fern Roget. "Call me when she gets there. Thank you for calling." She hung up.

Chapter 34

Todd and Roy reviewed the list of everyone who had access to the Control Room. Only the ten task force members, who were sworn to secrecy, the Chief, Roy and Todd comprised the group. It was obvious that Lily was the "leaker". The Chief did not realize that what he discussed with his dear wife went from her mouth to Jack's ears and as a result Todd and the Chief agreed to set up a misinformation agenda.

Todd asked the Chief to tell Lily that information on the possible ferryman's hideout had been received. Hopefully, that would spike him. The Chief's distress was apparent especially as he realized that his wife's gossiping to Jack most likely had aided their hunted monster. Todd assured the Chief that his lovely wife had no idea that her juicy chatter might help the killer.

The Chief and Todd were about to leave for a late lunch when Roy called the Chief. "This is Roy, Chief, need to speak to Todd, sir, put the call on the speaker phone, sir." "Sure Roy, go ahead." "Todd, Chief, we just got a red phone call. There's a possibility the Roget's daughter, Carolina, has gone missing. Fern Roget stated the high school principal called her this morning to tell her that Carolina was not in school. He called again at noon. Mrs. Roget mentioned to Mr. Durkin that her daughter wasn't happy in the school system and had threatened to go and live with her older sister in New York. She further said her daughter was very spoiled, narrow minded, devoted to herself and didn't participate in family affairs. The Mother went on to say that Carolina was in the worst of those teenage years. She has been calling her daughter, California but no Carolina has showed up. Mrs. Roget stated she fears Carolina might be a victim of those dreadful disappearances. That's it bosses, I'm awaiting orders."

Todd began pacing back and forth. The Chief moved over to his desk chair and watched and listened as Todd spoke on the phone. "Okay Roy, take two task force people with you and go immediately to the Roget's. Do your interviews but keep it low key. Secondly Roy, check train and bus travel, may be a record of her leaving Montauk. Third Roy, check the cab companies and ferries, she might have gone to a friend's. Fourth, check with the airlines and run a credit check on her card. How old is she? Okay, get a list from her parents of her friends and teachers. Interview all of them; give that job to the task force. And last, Roy, find out if she was a drug user. She might be right here in Montauk stoned out of her head. Oh and Roy, check to see on quick pass if she used the bridges. One more thing Roy, have a task force check particularly with the Block Island Ferry and all private and charter boat Captains. If she left Montauk we'll find her." "Yes sir, anything else, Lieutenant?" "That's it for now. Keep us updated on you findings Roy." "Roger that Todd, over and out." "You're right on it, Lieutenant!" praised the Chief.

Roy worked the phones as he organized everything into operation mode. Detective Eddie Di Roma and Sergeant Dick Di Roma were chosen to accompany Roy to the Roget's residence. The two brothers and Sergeant Roy Thompson arrived at 3:00pm and rang the doorbell on the exclusive red brick entrance. The butler, dressed in black with a white tie, opened the door and with his head lowered slightly and in a matter of fact tone, said, "I presume you are Sergeant Thompson, East Hampton Police?" "Yeah, that's me," and nodding at the brothers, "and Detectives Ed and Dick Di Roma. We're here to see Mr. and Mrs. Roget." "Yes, yes," replied the butler, "they are presently having afternoon tea and square sandwiches out on the patio.

Please wait until I announce your presence. They don't take kindly to being disturbed during their tea time." Annoyed, Roy asked, "oh yeah, well, where should we wait?" "Please sir," as he gestured to the brick walk, "there's a gate at the end where I will meet you, then I'll escort you gentlemen to the Roget's," he added for affect, "Please be patient with them, they're very upset about their daughter......." "What's your name," interrupted Roy. "Oh I am so sorry sir; it's Jason sir." "Okay Jason, we'll meet you at the gate."

Roy, Dick and Ed walked over to the gate entrance. "So guys, what do you think of the Roget's, they're very upset about their daughter's disappearance but they are having tea and sandwiches overlooking the lake?" Both Di Roma brothers smiled; Dick, remarking, "They will no likely flaunt their concerns in all modesty but they really don't give a damn." "How do you know that, Dick?" "Because Roy, three years ago I came here to investigate their daughter California's missing circumstances and guess what? I found her in the city, in the village, through credit card check. She implied she was never coming back to those assholes."

Another world, eh fellas," commented Dick as they walked to their police car. "Yeah, got that right, I know they're a lot of different kinds of people in Montauk, but those two are something else," answered Roy. And as he slammed the door of his cruiser, he said, "We might just as well have been talking to the parents of people who get an emotional relief when a child goes missing. They were annoyed by our presence guys, right?" "How did you like it Roy when they put their so called "faith" into a hearty laugh saying she'd be back because of the money?" asked Eddie. "Yeah, and they didn't even know one of her friends." Dick inquired, "By the way, what the hell are square sandwiches, Roy?" Roy and Eddie shrugged their shoulders.

Detective Ed Di Roma philosophized and offered, "a faculty given to people to conceal their inner thoughts." "Now, what the hell does that mean, Eddie?" asked Roy. "It means that in other words they mirrored the true feelings of their dark souls toward their daughter's disappearance or to put it bluntly Roy they don't give a damn!" "Yeah, now I see what you're talking about, Ed," as he pressed the accelerator hard, almost to the floor. "Maybe one day, I'll get them in a speed trap and I will, and I mean, I will, make their day." All three had a good, long knee- slapping chuckle.

The following day Todd, Roy and the Chief sat in an unmarked car and observed Lily entering Jack's. One and a half hours later they appeared at the doorway as Jack, the charming gentleman, held the door open for Lily. It seemed that the two had dished the dirt right up to the end. When Lily exited, they both smiled knowingly, evidently full of fat gossip.

Jack was anxious to whisper his new, juicy morsels of tidbits into everyone's ears. Not only was he a special member of the task force now but he was also known as the team's unofficial informer. The Chief looked at Todd, "Son if this strategy works and we outwit this psycho, I'm going to take Lily to Ireland for a vacation. She hasn't seen her sister in three years." Roy shot in, "How about us, Chief, we could use a vacation, too, when we nab this nut?" "Sure son, you both are wel-come to come along. Roy, her sister has a fine lass of a daughter, you know, a real red head with a few freck-les, one damn good farm gal she is, a bit overweight but the tastiest of cooks and a fine seamstress." Roy felt under an obligation and wished he had kept his mouth shut, but replied, "Sure Chief, that's just what I'm wishing for." Looking in his rear view mirror, Todd caught Roy's blushing bewilderment.

Back at Headquarters, Todd and Roy checked in their Control Center. The task force had completed their current jobs; nothing as usual. Once again Todd reviewed his charts as Roy once again was about to ramble on in his dejected tone. Todd raised his hand to stop Roy dead in his tracks, "I know Roy and to use your favorite word, NOTHING!" "That's it Todd, you took the word right out of my mouth." "Let's call it a day, Roy; we both need to get a good night's rest. We need to refuel. As my law professor liked to explain, "There's an inordinate, intense desire for declaring that when things go badly, man has a noble temptation to declare that all is going well." "Shit, Todd, that's great, so I'll just go around saying to myself, all is swell. The when I believe it, that's when I'll trip and fall into the lion's pad and ask Daniel how are you doing buddy, all going well?" "Okay Roy, you're real tired, let's get out of here."

Chapter 35

Calvin finished breakfast. It was time to pick up a one Mrs. Di Palma at the Nursing Home. Nathan had called the night before to inform Calvin that she was cooling off in the freezer and would be ready at 4:00am. They agreed this time on a fifty-fifty split of the Medicaid money.

Following the same procedure Calvin packed up Mrs. Di Palma as he had done with Mrs. Flannagan. Once she was tucked nicely away in the back seat of his truck, he camouflaged her with his fishing gear and nets. He inspected his work and thought, good, Mrs. Di Palma, you're set for your appointment out at the canyon with Mrs. Flannagan. Closing the rear door and hopping into the driver's seat he felt less nervous than last time. How odd doing this insane thing a second time and not having as many jitters as he had with Mrs. F; oh well, he mused and drove off before sunrise.

Cary and Calvin put in a long day. Calvin's was extra lengthy due to his early morning secret cruise to the canyon. The fishing proved exceptional and their freezer was filled with a mixture of makos, tiger and blue fin tuna. Dusk was approaching and Cary was ever so vigilant of those crazy kayaks, canoes and rubber wet-suitors in their array of crafts, sailing in the elbow by the Lighthouse. They had the right to be there but posed a great danger to both incoming and private charter boats that were returning at the end of the day. Cary's eyes scammed every inch of water it seemed as "Shark Killer II" plowed through the surf at thirty knots.

She spotted him in the high pitch wave; a wet suitor in his black outfit. He appeared to be straight ahead in the white wash of the wave. Cary turned the helm hard to leeward and heard Calvin yell, "Woman, what in God's name are you doing?" She, too, yelled, "Cal, Cal there is a wet suitor out bow front holding on to the end of his fishing pole." Shouting at the top of her lungs to be heard over the engine and water slapping against the helm, she continued, "Cal, he's bouncing up and down on the outgoing waves like he's riding a bronco; he's hanging on for dear life. He seems to be anchored to the bottom, but who knows how much longer that line is going to hold!" Cary stopped a moment to catch her breath. Yelling again, "Cal, if he breaks lose, he's a goner, Cal, no way are we going to find him in this gray hooded twilight, especially in that black suit." Cary thought for sure that this would certainly test her seamanship skills to the limit.

Calvin grabbed the life ring which had a one hundred foot, one inch nylon line attached to it. Shouting up to Cary, he yelled, "Get as close to him as you possibly can but keep a safe distance, I don't want him winding up in the props." He ran up front onto the bow while Cary caught another glimpse of the wet suitor on top of the wash. She turned port to pull up along side of him as Calvin, from the top of the bow, saw him in a downward rolling wash. Cal roared, "throttle down Cary, I'll throw him the ring as we pass." Cary throttled back as they slipped by him. He was still holding his pole and rising up and down in the brink. Judging the distance accurately, Calvin threw the ring twenty feet in front of his target allowing for the wave action to push it directly into his path.

They both watched anxiously as the wet suitor grabbed the moving ring. As he released his pole he waved thankfully. Calvin hauled him in the stern of the boat, pulled open the stern rear door so that the very appreciative fellow could climb down into the boat. Calvin could see how exhausted he was from the ordeal and had to help him on board.

Cal smiled at the lad, "Hi, I'm Cap Calvin and that's my mate, Cary." The grateful lad replied, "Hi, I'm Joshua, thank you for saving my life. I was at the end of my strength. You sure renewed my hopes when I saw you pulling up along side me." "What happened, lad?" "It's really dumb. A large wave came at me, I was standing on the outer rock off the bluffs and it passed by quietly but when it hit the beach it kind of reshaped coming back at me, I guess. I was keeping my eyes straight forward and then suddenly it slammed into my back and off I went with it, pulling me out nearly a hundred feet, I'd say, then the currents took me. I put a three ounce buck tail on my line and lowered it to the bottom but it snagged on a rock and held there for dear life. I prayed I wouldn't wind up in someone's propeller. I had a few near misses since no one was up at the helm, you know, when they have it on auto pilot. Anyway, I never thought I was going to make it."

"How are you feeling now, dear," asked Cary. "Could use a cup of coffee, some food and a blanket; been out there eight hours," Joshua answered. "In fact, I know that when we get back, my wife will cook you up the best corned beef and cabbage you ever had. It's her grandmother's recipe from Dublin." Cary's wide smile showed her delight as she said, "We sure in hell accept that invitation," and watched Cal as he shook his head in approval.

When the news of Joshua's rescue spread through the village, Cary and Calvin were hailed as heroes. It was the kind of respite that the townsfolk needed.

Chapter 36

He watched as the white SUV pulled up slowly into the small parking lot off East Lake Drive and came to a halt at the walking station next to the Blue and Green Trail charts. Karlton was most familiar with these trails and had enjoyed walking them for the past twenty years. He was an expert photographer and water colorist of wild life. His paintings reflected his photographs.

Karlton decided to walk along the Blue Trail to Little Reed Pond where he would find a variety of water fowl activity. He knew the beautiful morning light would be magnificent for shooting. Excited and filled with anticipation, he got out of his truck, opened the back door and gathered his equipment.

He held his three inch round walking stick tightly. His backpack was filled with all the appropriate apparatus. As he walked off the trail and on to the parking lot his walking stick kept pace with his quick steps. Unobserved, he came up behind Karlton, raised his stick, tapped him lightly on this shoulder and exclaimed heartily, "Top of the morning to you sir, I'm Sean O'Reilly, another perfect day, isn't it? We're surely fortunate men to be in paradise!"

Surprised and delighted at such a cheery welcome, Karlton replied exuberantly, "Top of the morning to you, too, lad. I'm Karlton Campbliss, off to Little Reed Path." "Blimey, I'm heading that way myself and if we're lucky we may be in for some special treats this morning." "That's what I'm hoping for, Sean. I first photograph the water fowl then put them on canvas. I do water colors of them." "Good for you, Karlton, do you sell them?" "I do exhibit my art work at the Railroad Depot; lots of Montauk artists display their work there." "I'll have to check it out." Karlton turned to his truck and commented, "I live on a small pension but my art work supplements it handsomely." He reached for his black Nikon carrying bag containing his 8.1 megapixel digital camera, his field spotting scope, tripod and a light weight portable chair. Sean offered to carry his bag. "I really need to get a bag with wheels;

it'll cost about fifty dollars." Sean eased the strap of Karlton's bag on to his shoulder and off they went.

The winding sandy trail was edged with tall reeds and cattails. Pine and shade trees were sprinkled at random. Some wild flowers were still in bloom especially the golden rod. All was quiet and soft with no signs of human interruption. The two men chatted congenially as they paced along the path.

"I saw a pair of skunks and one good size fox here last week," Sean informed Karlton. "Oh, up at Big Reed Path yesterday there were two beavers, a sharp-skinned hawk and a pair of red tail hawks, Sean. Surely this park is the habitat of numerous birds and animal life and water fowl and being an artist, for me, this area is like a zoological garden!" "You're right. Karl, I can believe that." "Did you know Sean, that there are two types of ducks?" "Sure, Karl, there are diving and paddling ducks. You know, flock behavior and wing beat both help to distinguish one species from another." "Right you are. I observed, over the years, that mallards, pintails and wideons form loose group maneuvers whereas teal and shovelers flash by in small, compact bunches. Now, canvasbacks shift from waving lines to temporary vees."

Sean listened intently as the old artist rambled loquaciously on and appreciated the fact that he was very knowledgeable of water fowl life. In fact, Sean admired a man who was so interested in duck life. "Not all ducks quack, Sean," Karlton explained. "Many ducks whistle, squeal or grunt and the sounds of their wings also help to identify them." Pointing to a red winged black bird, Sean remarked, "That guy and the Baltimore oriole almost outshine the red cardinal beauty wise, you know." "Yes, I would have to agree with you on that, Sean. Well, another two tenths of a mile and we'll get to Little Reed Pond," Karlton informed his chum.

"As I was saying, my friend, although not a hard and fast rule, different species tend to use different types of habitats. For instance, paddle ducks like shallow marshes and creeks while divers prefer larger and more open waters." The long-winded Karlton continued, "Most ducks shed their feathers twice a year and nearly all ducks lose their plumage after mating and for a few weeks resemble females."

As they rounded the curve in the trail Little Reed Pond came into view at one tenth of a mile ahead. "Only another five minutes 'til we reach water," announced Sean. "Yes, and by the way, any ducks feeding in croplands will likely be a paddler for most of this group is sure footed and can walk and run very well on land. Their diet is vegetables and grain so we know why mallards and pintails are good tasting birds for humans."

Once they reached the pond, Karlton set up his equipment. Without realizing his environmental lesson, so to speak, was over, he told Sean how upset he was about the recent vanishings in Montauk. "What do you think about these killings, Sean?" Shrugging his shoulders, Sean answered, "He's more than likely a druggie who needs money for his next fix."

Have you noticed all the wild turkeys around here, Karl?" "Well, a week ago Sean, I saw a long eared owl, a pair of short eared owls and a northern saw owl." "Look, see, there's a pair of gadwells about to land on the water." Karlton started to click away. "Hey," Sean called, "off to your right, look, a pair of blue winger teals." Karlton estactic, turned and clicked some more. Out of the reeds came a flock of mallards, swimming out to deeper water, ever so often tipping up to feed. Suddenly, to the left, two canvas backs splashed down in a soft landing. An exuberant Karleton snapped away.

Sean moved on closer to the water and as he pointed down into the water he exclaimed, "Look at all that bait!" Karlton walked over and hunched down in order to see better. He felt the blow crushing his collar bone. The impact forced him into the water. Sean placed his foot on Karlton's back and held his head in the water with the back of his walking stick. He watched as the bubbles reached the surface, making a strange popping sound at their journey's end. When the bubbles stopped surfacing after thirty seconds or so he turned Karlton over and noticed his red face was turning to a red purple hue. His eyes were wide open with a surprised long farewell look. Sean took the body bag from his knapsack and placed Karlton inside. He walked back along the trail ever alert for human activity.

Upon reaching the parking lot he was relieved to see only Karlton's SUV. He headed for the large berm, slid the bag into the pre-creviced location, walked quickly through the woods, reached the road, looked both ways, dashed across it and reached his truck parked among the daily vehicles at Dick Calf's lot. He drove back, hopped out of his truck, walked to the berm, retrieved the body bag and hid it under the black canvas in his truck's tailgate. "Oh Karlton, I forgot to tell you, I also saw a pair of chocolate minks this morning but I guess you don't really care. Oh well.............

Later that morning, the Merrits pulled up along-side of Karlton Campbliss' SUV. Margaret Merrit re-marked, "Karlton must be down at Little Reed Pond, let's go visit him, he's such an interesting man." "Sure hon," agreed Wesley. They took their backpacks and their walking sticks and headed down the winding trail most anxious to meet their friend and fellow nature lover at his favorite spot.

Twenty minutes later they were at the last bend on the path and after another fifty yards stopped to stare at Karlton's bird watching gear. "That's strange hon; where the hell is he? I can't imagine he'd leave his expensive equipment and walk off." "Wesley, see here? It's his field scope, his name is engraved on it," explained Margaret in an anxious voice. "I have a bad feeling about this Wesley, let's get out of here." "Right hon."

Scared to death they managed to return to their truck. Once inside, Wesley slammed the car door locks, started the truck, moved to the front lot and parked. He opened his cell phone and punched in 911 and reported his concerns to the dispatcher. Thank-ing him and giving instructions to wait at the front en-trance until the police arrived was all they could offer at this time. Wesley and Margaret sat speechless and thought how close they had come to another possible disappearance.

Chapter 37

Todd had given the guys a day off. Now he knew there would be lots for him to do at his liquor store. Wine and liquor orders needed to be placed again, checks had to be mailed; a never ending mound of paper work. As soon as he had completed his task his cell phone rang. "Hi, what's up, Roy? "It's happened again, Todd. It appears a one Mr. Karlton Campbliss has gone missing. A couple, Wesley and Margaret Merritt found Karlton's bird watching equipment down at Blue Trail where it ends at Little Reed Pond. No sign of Karlton." "Roy, get the dog team and forensics up there." "They're on their way as we speak. Pick you up in ten minutes, okay?" "Okay Roy, see you in ten."

Damn, what am I missing here? Todd rewound the tape in his mind and added the new episode. He's now doubled back to the third missing person's scene.

One and two were like that, three was a set up, four and five occurred on the south side, six is still up in the air and now number seven takes place where number three disappeared. This psycho is all over the place yet seems to go about his business sight unseen; right in plain sight. Or is he getting desperate? Is he now willing to take chances? That's it; our presence is got to be putting the pressure on him. He knows the noose is getting tighter. He's exposing himself to greater risks with each new missing person. Normally, one would go into hiding; keeping low. Not this guy, he's becoming brasher and that has to lead to his downfall. His unpredictability is catching up to him. I say he's coming to the end of the maze and doesn't know which way to turn. This uncertainty will force him to gamble. Look at today, he took a mighty big chance in an open park with nature lovers all over the place. He took a hundred to one shot. Here is a gamester tottering on the edge. I'll be there when you fall Mr. Ferryman. I'm going to haul your ass in. Not unexpectedly, but breaking his thought pattern, Todd realized the wailing sound coming form the back of his store was Roy. He locked up and joined his buddy in the cruiser.

As soon as they arrived at the park they went directly to the scene down at Little Reed Pond in a golf cart provided by the County Park officials. While Todd talked to his task force people, Roy took an inventory of the bird watching gear and called the East Hampton Camera Shop to get prices on each item. When Todd finished with the task force he and Roy returned to the golf cart, sat down and reviewed Roy's information. "Here goes, Todd: one Nikon digital camera, $729.00, a Nikon files scope, $129.99, tripod, $279.00, seat, $199.00 and a bag at $95.00. That's a total of $1431.99, Todd. He's not interested in any of the victims' belongings, just the quarry. Strange, but that's his MO and he sticks to it except in Carolina's case; no missing person scene plus all of her belongings vanished along with her. You know Todd, I believe he didn't plan that one; he just came upon her like a, hm-mmm, you know, a hitch hiker."

"That's it, Roy, she was hitching hiking out of town and he came along, saw her, most likely early in the morning, did her in his vehicle and took her wherever he takes them. Roy, you're going to make detective yet, smart thinking pal." "Thanks buddy. Now, did forensics come up with anything?" "They found what appears to be a face print in the mud at the edge of the pond. We're assuming he drowned him there. The dog teams and search parties came up empty, Roy, therefore, he either carried him out or had a small inflatable craft to ferry him away. Let's get out of here, Roy, I want to inform the Chief and add new information to my ferryman theory. When forensics rap things up here they'll report to you." Roy, put the golf cart in drive and they crawled back up to Blue Trail and to their police cruiser.

Chapter 38

It was 9:30am, two days since Karlton Campbliss met his fate. Nothing seemed to make sense not even the sun casting shadows of golden rays over the tormented village on this October day. Roy was engrossed with all the task force reports while Todd was putting some finishing touched on his ferryman chart.

"Hey Roy," Todd shouted, "Roy I got it!" Sitting straight up, Roy said, "What the hell have you got?" "His pattern Roy, his pattern. Put yourself in his shoes. Where does that lead?" Roy thought for a quick moment, "No where. I don't know, Todd. I'm not a John Jay graduate. What patterns?" "He's keeping to his antiquity of error, he's sticking to his human force of error." "Todd, what the hell are you talking about?" "How's this, Roy, we all form habits and eventually habits form us, right?" "Okay, Todd, I can go along with that but what behavior pattern is he following?" "Roy, think about it. One and two were done at the same site." "Yeah, okay, so?" "So Roy, he does seven at three's site." "Yeah so?" "Don't you see it, Roy, he's going back to the locations he feels most comfortable about, and, so, Roy, it's bingo. He's going to show up at one of these areas again. I want immediate 24-7 surveillance of all three sites; tabletop, the County Park and the south side." "Shit, Todd, you're good. You got all this from your theory chart?" "Yes Roy, what the hell do you think I've been working on for the past few weeks?"

Roy called the task force to set up coverage. He also spoke to Sergeant Steve Hotchkiss of the State Park Police at the local Montauk office. "Okay, Roy, I'll make my presence known on the south side," he assured Roy. Roy thanked him and added, "This might be our breakthrough, Steve. We need to nab this psycho fast." "Roger that Roy out."

Sergeant Hotchkiss assigned Mannie to do the night tour while he would conduct the day surveillance before further orders were received from Headquarters at Jones Beach. Wasting no time, Steve drove his jeep to the park entrance, made a right into Camp Hero and continued up the pot-filled road until he reached the main parking lot.

No fishermen, no campers or trucks; the lot was empty. It was uncommonly quiet for this time of year. Normally, surfcasters hunting for big bass and blues packed this spot. The disappearances had put an end to many activities. Montauk's dark side prevailed. No anglers wanted to deal with the impending doom lurking in the hamlet. She was no longer a Mecca for the fishermen seeking out the most exciting and heart pounding striped bass or blue fishing ever. Steve thought, she's becoming a ghost town; the parking lots are empty, no one is visiting the Lighthouse or picnicking in the state parks. The situation is really getting out of hand, he felt, but, as long as I get my paycheck each week, I can do what I've been trained to do.

Steve eased his jeep down the old bumpy road until he reached the designated parking station where anglers would park their vehicles and walk to their favorite fishing locals. In fact, he knew this was the area where Reese and Elizabeth disappeared. As he drove around the bend he spied a black truck parked in a handicapped parking space. There appeared to be a man sitting in the driver's seat and no handicapped sticker. Steve pulled directly behind him and turned on his lights. Sure enough, thought Steve, it was a male in his late forties. He turned off the ignition, stepped out of his jeep and put on his round gray trooper's hat.

Posturing his best official look as he swaggered to the driver's door, he said, "Excuse me sir, you're parked in a handicapped parking lane without the proper plate or sticker." The driver was irritated by the officer's high pitched arrogant voice and thought what an asshole this guy is; so full of himself in his superman's uniform. Looking straight out unto the ocean he remarked, "Officer, I just finished my lunch and there's no one down here and besides these two handicapped lanes allow one an ocean view. It's a beautiful day. I didn't think anybody would mind and if handicapped people show up, I would most certainly move my truck."

In a more commanding voice, Steve said, "Where's your Camp Hero Parking Permit, it's required by New York State law, you know?" Now he began to feel even more provoked and turning his head directly toward the short, overweight park policeman, replied, "Excuse me, what's a Camp Hero Permit?" "It's a permit you purchase at the Montauk Downs State office. It costs $50.00 and allows one entry into Camp Hero and its parking privileges." He thought, I would like to pound this twit into the ground like a nail into wood. "Sir, under New York State law not only are you required to have a Camp Hero Permit but you must have fishing equipment such as a fishing pole, lures, waders, etc. on your person."

His dislike for this officer turned into a cold repugnance. He hated authority especially coming from a lack-witted simpleton; give them a badge and poof they become lord and master. "What's your name sir?" "Sean O'Reilly," the driver answered. "Sean, your vehicle's right taillight is broken; that's a vehicular violation. New York State law requires all automobiles must be in proper road working order."

Sean's short temper was about to erupt. He recalled his hatred of authoritative people as he remembered how his elementary teachers used to swat him with a wooden pointer if his appearance didn't meet with their approval or God forbid his homework was not up to snuff. They were egotistical people of low taste and more interested in them selves than in him. I'll put an end to this guy's high and mightiness, Sean decided, as he snapped open the door and pushed Officer Hotchkiss two feet forward almost knocking him off balance.

Regaining his footing, Officer Hotchkiss exclaimed, "Sir I did not give you permission to exit your truck." Sean, towering over the pudgie, short officer, commented, "You're not my father, I sure in hell don't need your permission," as he walked to the rear of his truck and inspected his broken tail light. "I have a roll of red duct tape in my glove compartment; it'll make it as good as new." Steve Hotchkiss held his ground, "No way sir, New York State law requires you must replace broken tail lights with a new manufacturer's specified light for your vehicle. Mr. O'Reilly, I am not permitted by New York State law to allow you to do a temporary fix. So I have to write you up on all three vehicle violations."

Sean stared down at this presumptuous "wanna be" and determined this idiot, with his audacious tongue of vanity needed to learn a lesson in humility. He planned to kill him and thought, that's another New York State law I'll be violating! Officer Hotchkiss stuck out his right hand and in a loud, demanding tone asked to see Sean's license and registration. Nodding, Sean reached through the window and lowered the visor and handed both to the officer. He inspected said items, looked up at Sean in a surprised manner, "Sir you referred to yourself as Sean O'Reilly, these don't match that name." "Look Officer Hotchkiss, the truck and license belong to my partner. I just borrowed his truck; my wallet is in my briefcase." "Sir New York State law forbids you from driving a vehicle under an assumed license; that's number four."

Sean was boiling mad. He shouted, "Okay, okay, write me up, that's what you do best, right Officer Hotchkiss?" "Quite right sir, I'll just run a check on your plate, stay put." Officer Steve Hotchkiss's mistake was to turn his back to Sean and as he walked briskly back to his jeep he heard three loud gun shots that ripped his chest with a fire that burned hot, angry pain. He started falling forward and saw three red gushing streams of blood flowing from his chest. He hit the ground stone dead.

Sean walked carefully over to Officer Hotchkiss so as not to step in any blood and felt his neck. There was no pulse. He put on his gloves, walked to the jeep and moved it along side of his truck. He then retrieved both the license and registration from the officer's right hand, rolled him over, bent down and opened his gun belt. I could use another Glock pistol and ammunition, he thought, it's no use to you, Officer Hotchshit!

Sean climbed back into his truck, replaced his license and registration behind the visor and tucked the gun belt under his seat. He turned his ignition on, the engine roared to life and the truck proceeded cautiously up the bumpy road.

When he reached the upper parking lot, he slammed on his brakes, stopped his vehicle and just sat there. I had not planned on this. My killings are organized; there is a purpose to them. This is unacceptable, he yelled to himself in his truck cab. Becoming so out-raged he punched his large fist into the steering wheel. That fastidious little hump made me do a foolish, in-sane and reckless killing! Now they will triple their efforts to find me, just what I need; more manpower on the prowl. That SOB, he shouted, as he bashed his fist into the instrument panel, scattering glass down on to the rubber floor mat. Get a hold of yourself, he scolded, and took a few breaths. No doubt this event is a setback but I'll learn from it. Life is full of surpris-es. I'll turn this obstacle into my full advantage. Just because hotshot is dead it doesn't change a thing, still have more to do. I need more to disappear and when I kill there is a full proof plan for the disposals. As a matter of fact, my system is working out better than I could have hoped. Feeling calmer and smug, he drove off and returned to his safe harbor.

Chapter 39

Sergeant Phillip Sheridan of the Jones Beach State Park Police was trying to reach Sergeant Steve Hotchkiss. Sergeant Sheridan knew Hotchkiss pulled the 8:00am to 4:00pm shift; Private Forsythe manned the 4:00pm to midnight and Private Devin finished out until 8:00am. It was now 1:00pm and Hotchkiss was overdue for his routine hourly check in. Sergeant Sheridan ran a tight ship; his rules must be followed. What was really unsettling was the lack of communication between Sheridan and Hotchkiss. Steve was not responding to Sheridan's radio calls so the Sergeant figured okay, radio malfunction, but, the fact that he didn't answer his state back up cell phone was highly unusual. Hotchkiss knows the correct procedure, Sheridan thought, so why hadn't he got his ass to a phone and called he wondered. Rules were established for one's safety and since he was now fifteen minutes late it's not going to look good on his record, Sheridan further deduced. He knew he had to cover his own ass since he was due for promotion to Lieutenant. Okay, Sheridan decided, I'll have to red flag you, Hotchkiss. An officer in distress was serious business and Sheridan knew it would be better to let Lieutenant Gragg make the call.

Gragg instructed Sheridan to have Todd's task force check out their situation since they were the closest to the park in Montauk. Sheridan called Roy and informed him of the dilemma and asked for immediate assistance. Roy stated they would comply and would report back as soon as they could make a determination of Hotchkiss' status. A grim faced Sergeant Roy Thompson hung up the phone. Todd noted his expression and right away speculated that there was another vanishing. Roy filled him in on the urgent request from Sergeant Sheridan as the two left the Control Center for their cruiser.

Racing at full speed up to the State Park, Todd, in deep thought, never seemed to notice their speed. They were a half mile from the entrance to Camp Hero when out of nowhere, like a thunderbolt, the task force lead detective, Sergeant Danny Foster's voice roared over the air waves, "Officer down, officer down, code blue, Montauk Fire Department requests ambulance." He continued with the location, "south side lower parking lot." Todd snatched his mike, firing in to it, "Danny, who's down, over." "Todd, it's Sergeant Hotchkiss sir, he appears to be dead sir. He took three bullets in the back, Todd. They exited his chest, over."

Stunned silence filled the cruiser. Both officers felt a sick feeling of nausea welling up in their stomachs. Their minds shut down temporarily as the shock of the Sergeant's death was overwhelming. Todd regained his focus and thought the disappearances are one thing but a fellow officer lying on his back with three bullet holes in his chest was quite another matter. Todd heard Danny's far off monotone sounds repeating, "Lieutenant, Todd, sir, Todd sir, Todd." Almost in slow motion, Todd squeezed the end on his mike, "Danny, what is you exact location, over?" "Sir we're on the bottom trail where the two Hawkins missing person's scene is situated, over." "Danny, get forensics up there and don't let the ambulance crew touch him, over" "Yes sir, over."

Roy slowed down as they entered Camp Hero and drove to the top of the rough trail leading down to the crime scene. They exited the cruiser and walked to where Danny and Tom Collins were standing. Todd observed their solemn expressions and the struggle in their eyes; the look that faced the hateful scene of a fallen officer. Roy, staring at Hotchkiss' lifeless body, became weak-kneed and sickened from the sight. His parched throat begged for water. Todd made one final inspection of his deceased comrade after the ambulance crew arrived and together he and Roy returned to their cruiser where Roy gulped down an entire bottle of water. The crime scene now belonged to the forensic team's crew.

"How are you feeling, buddy?" asked Todd as Roy drove at 30mph back to town. "Like shit, Todd, twelve years on the force I thought hardened me to almost anything but I was ready to faint back there." "Roy, no matter how long you're on the force you never get used to a scene like this." "No way, Todd, is this the work of our ferryman; he takes bodies, doesn't use a gun and by the way I noticed that Hotchkiss' gun belt was missing. Our creep doesn't take things, he leaves things." Listening carefully to Roy's evaluation, Todd put his hand on his forehead, rubbed it and closed his eyes and thought.

Hotchkiss was only twenty four years old, with the state force for three years, lived at home with his mother, father and two younger brothers. He was bright, passed the Sergeant's test in three years, had a good career potential and no doubt would have made it to the top. "It's the ferryman, Roy, that I'm damned sure." "Now what in hell leads you to that direction, Todd? It sure ain't his MO; he doesn't operate in this mode. It's not his style, Todd." "Theoretically you're right, Roy, but ask yourself Roy, who else could have done it? It fits my pattern theory, Roy. I surmise he returned to a site in which he was comfortable, perhaps, setting up a new field operation. It's the nature of things, Roy, plans don't always shape up the way you think they will. Circumstances change and he reacts to them. We could go through all the working hypothesis in the world, buddy, but this is his work. I have no doubt about it. This is no supposition Roy, this is fact. Why did he use a pistol this time, Roy? Easy, he was caught off guard. He reacted according to the situation as it unfolded and my best guess is that Steve, most likely, had taken his license and registration, probably was about to run his plate or write up a ticket. And Roy, when Steve turned to walk back to his jeep that's when he took him out." "Why did he take Steve's gun belt?" "Why wouldn't he, Roy? He's a killer and a new Glock and ammo might come in handy one day. It's a trade off, Roy, killers don't always reason things out, they just respond to events as they go along, and, yes, Roy, he plans but he didn't plan on this."

Forensic reports were sent the very next morning. Todd and Roy went through the information carefully. The only relative items were the two smashed bullets, shot from a Glock pistol, that were found in a tree after they exited Hotchkiss' chest. Todd had expected this disappointing news but had an idea that he posed to Roy. "Just on a hunch Roy, check all personal police records, state, county and town. Verify one way or another if someone lost a Glock pistol. Check with arms dealers to see if they have a record of anyone who purchased a Glock within the last twenty years." "Am on it Lieutenant."

He felt the pressure now from the authorities. His nefarious activities would have to be executed with far more precaution. He was especially exasperated after the Hotchkiss disaster and concluded that he would have to move in a new direction, away from their prying eyes and constant patrols. Going to the market was getting to be a problem with the vigilant surveillance. He needed two more bodies badly.

Considering a previous idea, he began to plot with his usual maniacal intent that led him to a different and more secure location. No doubt, he was aware of the unpredictability involved, but assumed that with expert planning, he would achieve his goal. His main obstacle was to figure out a way in which he could enter and leave a particular building without being seen. Once that was resolved he would schedule his new event. He popped open a bottle of spring water, took a gulp, and began to organize his offense.

Chapter 40

Nathan Cain was immersed in the kind of administrative paperwork he savored. He hid his government transactions and never shared them with his accounting department. The elaborate set of phony books he created was responsible for the bountiful harvest of Medicaid monies. For sure, the government auditors were sharp but what they didn't realize was that Nathan had fabricated a series of false paper trails and had all the back up documents to support his bogus presentation. He crossed checked and double checked and disguised it all so well that the government sharpies never questioned or flagged his accounts. Nathan took pride in his ability to outsmart them and relished his role as the perfectly honest hypocrite. He thirsted for all that wonderful free government money. There was no cure for his greed.

After finishing his book work for the day, Nathan locked all his private matters safely away in his office vault. Just as he spun the combination around, the phone rang. "Yes, Mrs. Whitehall?" "Nathan, the Demiscos are here, their daughter and her husband are with them. Shall I bring them up?" "That will be fine, Mrs. Whitehall, thank you."

Mrs. Whitehall opened Nathan's heavy office door and escorted the Demiscos inside. Nathan, the gentleman that he was, stood erectly, in his navy blue pin striped suit and smiled warmly at them as if they were familiar family members. Holding out his hand and grasping Mrs. Demisco's hand, he exclaimed, "I presume you are Rose. My dear you look twenty years younger than what your file indicates you are! No way, are you and your husband, Jerry in your nineties!" Right on cue, Mrs. Whitehall added. "It must be a typo, sir, I'll have it checked." Rose Demisco remarked, "Oh, you're so the kidder, Mr. Cain." "Please call me Nathan, Rose." "There's no need to check the records," chirped Mrs. Demisco, "I'll be ninety two in December and Jerry will be ninety in January." Nathan walked over to shake Jerry's hand, declaring, "How fit and healthy you both look!" That was a lie; he knew their medical history. They both had heart problems, their medication was extensive. Rose used a walker and Jerry rode around in a light gray wheel chair. '

Easing over to the daughter, Ines, Nathan reached for her hand and held it in both of his as he said glowingly, "You're as lovely as the day and I might add as fair as the rose in May. My, you have your Mom's pretty blue eyes and her dainty cute nose." Looking admiringly at her husband, "It's a pleasure to meet you, too, Terry. I understand you're a writer. Published any books?" "No, sir, I'm a master carpenter working for Montauk Services, Inc., on my time off I'm writing a mystery thriller." "Well, now, I'll be looking forward to an autographed copy, Terry." "Thanks, sir, I just completed chapter four. Writing is more difficult than I had thought but I'll manage, God willing." "Yes, son, God willing but be careful of the publishers, they're money hungry hawks. And speaking of hunger, why don't we all head over to the lunch room? My chef loves to serve a mid-morning snack, just a perfect little coffee and tea arrangement with sweet cakes." All agreed as Nathan's clever plan took shape.

They enjoyed their morning treats as Nathan pointed out the lush, beautiful flower garden and the private sitting area right outside the lunch room. He explained that there were two lunch rooms, a large formal dining room and four breakfast rooms, each decorated differently to give one a new setting to start their day. He had the gift of gab, knew how to play the game of circles and injected a few sweet raisins into his conversation.

Tom, the chef, showed up and introduced himself to the Demiscos, stating that whatever special meals they desired he would be delighted to accommodate. He explained how everyone was family at the home and that his food brought everyone even closer to to-gether. "My large staff and I are here to meet your ev-ery food fantasy," Tom quipped. As soon as his short act was over, he excused himself and returned to the kitchen to prepare the luncheon peanut butter and jel-ly sandwiches for the home's survivors. Various staff members and residents strolled by their table reassur-ing the Demiscos what a wonderful center Nathan ran. They all knew they would be rewarded for their sweet talk.

Nathan began the grand tour de force. It always proved to be his master stroke. He counseled them in such a charming manner and out maneuvered their every concern. After the tour they returned to the main lobby. Nathan turned to Mrs. Whitehall and suggested, "Why don't you take Rose and Jerry to the bingo room while Ines and Terry and I go to my of-fice? Bingo begins in ten minutes." With a twinkle in his eye and looking straight into Rose's light blue eyes, Nathan winked and said, "If you get the lucky cards, Rose, you could win one hundred dollars in paper money to be used in our gift shop!" This was just another one of Nathan's ploys since he arranged who would get the lucky cards. One could say that what went on at Nathan's stayed at Nathan's. Rose loved bingo and Jerry was a bingo caller at the church every Saturday night. Both followed Mrs. Whitehall very happily down the hall to the bingo room.

Nathan led Ines and Terry back to his office and delighted in the fact that this was when the real fun would begin. Furthermore he was more than confident since one of his greatest assets was his used car salesman spiel. He would outwit this naïve couple and sell them a line of crap they couldn't resist. Above all he was looking forward to their parent's fat Medicaid check.

As they entered his playroom, he thought, I'm the fox, they're the geese. This should prove sporting! Nathan began with a review of the Demisco's file commenting that it was time to make a decision. "We have a home away from home right here for them," he offered. "I realize at first it's hard for them to enter a new habitat but believe me they will adjust because we will give them the best of care and love." Ines replied softly, "I know, Nathan but they're like kids now and really don't trust anyone except us. We give them all the attention we can. Nathan, it's very difficult, caring for them is very demanding and we somehow manage. I know we need our space, too, but they're my parents and I know they don't want to be here and leave their home. They want to be with us and live in the house they have lived in for over forty years and continue to enjoy their comforts." In a twitter, Ines paused and asked nervously, "Oh Terry, what ever shall we do?"

Nathan shook his head up and down like an under-standing father, "Ines, I know how attached you are to your Mother and Father but don't you also think that both of you need a rest?" coaxed Nathan. "Now, my Center is state of the arts, we watch over our family as if they were our children. You were just on our tour; tell me, did you see anybody who seemed to be un-happy?" "No, Nathan," uttered Ines, "but I know my Mom's moods. Your staff, while meaning well, will not be able to read into my Mom's needs and it also really concerns me that my Mom and Dad's accommoda-tions here will not meet with their approval."

Nathan knew exactly where she was going with this. He had dealt with similar mother and daugh-ter relationships in the past. It was now time to play his trump card. "Look, kids, why don't you take some time off to think this through. How about Las Vegas?" Ines and Terry bolted straight up in their chairs, "Las

Vegas?" they both sputtered in bewilderment. "Sure, why not, get a load off your minds. Let me take care of your folks while you two live it up for two weeks at my condo in Vegas." "Oh, sir, we couldn't afford that, we are barely getting by now with taking care of my parents and ourselves." The "good Samaritan" told them how his mother had taught him to relish the luxury of being good to others and paused to allow them to digest the saintly but fictitious tale.

"I shall arrange for you and Terry to fly first class, stay in my condo and I will have $1,000 in comp chips for you at the MGM Grande. No expense to you, even the shows will be reserved in your name. Just go relax; you two deserve it!"

Terry was beside himself with excitement; Ines knew she needed a break. Nathan could see the thrill he had evoked on their faces. "So, it's a deal. Tomorrow you'll be off to the city of glitter and glitz and dear Mom and Dad will appreciate their stay here." "But Terry," wondered, Ines, "Will Montauk Services give you two whole weeks off?" "No problem, darling, let's go for it! And your Mom and Dad also need a vacation. They'll meet new people and play bingo, even work out a little and eat all that great food here that Tom will cook for them. They're two lucky ducks, if you ask me!" Ines nodded and almost smiled as she said, "We'll go, and, thank you, Nathan." "Great, now, you leave it all to me. Mrs. Whitehall will arrange to have a limo pick you up tomorrow morning. Hurry home now and pack!"

Jerry and Rose Demisco were thrilled for their daughter and her husband. To think that such a man would do such a wonderful thing delighted them and they agreed to stay in Nathan's Center, for after all, how could they refuse such a generous man's offer.

Chapter 41

Jack sat down placing his ever familiar full steam-ing coffee pot on the table where Todd and Roy were waiting for their lunch. Jack was in good spirits since this nasty business tripled his shop's income. "Your fish and chips will be ready soon guys," he announced cheerfully. "The best in the town, by far," he laughed. Todd asked, "Have you come up with any intelligence for the task force, Jack? We're depending on you, pal." Jack shrugged his shoulders, adding, "It's like the hush of death out there, nothing, just damn nothing." Roy piped up, "See, Todd, I'm not the only one who uses that word." "Right, Roy. Trust me you two our psycho is going down. He misplayed Hotchkiss; that was one big blunder number two; his next miscalculation will be his last. Like they say, three strikes and you're out." They all pondered that for a few moments. "Okay, Jack," Todd said, "If you hear anything of interest, call

Roy or me immediately, again we're counting on you, buddy." Puffed up, Jack stated point blank, "Roger that sir."

Fred rang the bell twice, signaling Jack their lunch was ready. Jack hopped up to the counter and returned with two baskets full of hot fish and chips which he placed carefully in front of his two special customers and wished them "bon appetite". In between bites, Todd asked Roy how the Glock tracing was going. Roy expressed his frustration, "Slow, Todd, I have the Di Roma brothers on it but to date no hits on missing police Glocks. By the end of the week they should be finished checking all State, County and Park personnel and Ed is in the process of compiling a list of arms dealers. All interviews and corresponding paper work is time consuming, Todd. You know, the Di Romas are experts in this area but they know to call me if they need assistance." "Good Roy, keep on top of it. If my hunch is right we're going to find this Glock carrying psychopath."

Jack was all ears as he absorbed his bosses' conversation. He was tickled pink to be once again in on a new developing task force strategy. He promised himself not to leak anything and lose Todd's confidence. Oops, he spotted some one holding up his empty coffee cup. He grabbed his pot, sent it aloft and hurried to refill the cup and thought, wow, what a day this has been.

Chapter 42

He had checked out the building two nights ago. He knew exactly where and how to enter it. He hid his truck behind the large dumpster. It was 3:00am; time to move and if all went according to plan his task would take about a half hour. Stepping out of his truck he walked guardedly to the maintenance entrance. Next to the door he had placed a square black milk crate instead of using a ladder which someone might have noticed. The old window he had chosen had eight six inch panes on the top and on the bottom and was locked with a normal window latch. He stepped up on the milk crate and used his glass cutter to cut the top half of the window's bottom pane next to the latch.

The glass cutter made simple work of his job, like a hot knife on butter. Next he tapped the circle of glass with his gloved hand; it sprinkled to the floor. He opened the latch, pushed up on the bottom half of the window, entered through the opening and lowered himself quietly to the maintenance room floor. He closed the window and fastened the latch.

He turned on his six inch flashlight and listened attentively as he walked to the back of the room. He opened the rear door, allowing him access into the main section of the building. He looked down the corridor; all was quiet. Like a cat on the hunt, he sprang across the hall to the stairway which led up to the various floors. Having memorized the building's blueprint at the library, he knew precisely where he was. Hurrying up the thirteen steps, he stopped at the fire exit door, opened it slowly and peered out. The hall lighting was dim, but, again all was clear. He reached the end of the hallway and found himself directly across from the room he had chosen.

Checking his watch at 3:10am, affirmed that he was well within his time frame. He darted across the hall and entered the room. As expected, they were sleeping. He thought it must be a husband a wife situation. A fuzzy night light gave him just enough of a glow to see clearly. He moved noiselessly toward a wheelchair and took the pillow off the seat. No need to club them now; the pillow will keep this clean. He lowered the pillow gently over the sleeping face and applied pressure. It was over faster than he could have imagined.

He felt the body go limp. Checking the neck for a pulse he found none. He held the pillow over the second person whom he assumed was the wife. He smothered her, too, in no time.

All of a sudden he heard some sort of noise. He walked quickly to the door, opened it a crack and looked down the hall and saw what looked like a night guard in the not too far distance checking patient's rooms. The guard would shine his flashlight into the room while he seemed to listen for a moment and then close the door. He's probably making sure they're still breathing, he thought. My two stopped breathing two minutes ago. This is not good, he felt. As the guard drew nearer, he prepared for action and stood behind the door holding his club high over his head.

Reno, a widower and a retired firefighter, enjoyed working nights. The extra money was good and he was well liked. He opened the next door, stood quietly and listened. Funny, I don't hear any of those sleepy sounds; better check. Aaaaah, these are the new old folks, he realized, as he glanced up at the door panel reading the names: Jerry Demisco, Rose Demisco. Reno took a short step to enter the room just as his hand held radio lighted up. A woman's voice said, "Reno, our dinner is ready; get your fat ass up here. I'm hungry, how 'bout you?" Reno held the radio up to his mouth and pushed the speaker button, "'Sally, I just want to check the new couple. I don't hear any of those sleep noises, over." "Reno, just get your damn ass up here, if they're dead they can wait dinner, I can't." "Sally, my dear, I think you just saved my life, I'm starving, be there in five," as he closed the Demisco's door.

He lowered his club, thinking, two's enough, don't need three. Checking his watch it was 3:25; time to get out of here. He put Jerry on his right shoulder and Rose on his left; feather weights, he remarked. He opened the door, peered up the corridor, saw Reno stepping into the elevator, watched the slow moving doors close, stepped out of the room and closed the door. He crossed the hallway, entered the stairwell and walked down to the maintenance room with his baggage in tow. He decided to use the maintenance door since it was self locking. As soon as the Demiscos were safely tucked under the canvas he drove off to his sanctuary.

After the late shift's dinner, Sally made out their guard status reports. Reno had noted in quotes, "no sleep sounds in room 125". He learned from the fire department to always cover your ass.

Chapter 43

Julia McPherson arrived at the Center promptly at 8:00 am every morning. As the head of the maintenance department she supervised twenty five employees. Julia was dedicated to her job and took pride in her punctuality.

On this rainy October morning, Julia opened the door to the maintenance room, shook the water off her umbrella and hung it on a nail. Some work orders needed her immediate attention and as she busied herself at her paper filled desk she realized that the soft sound she had been hearing in the background was the drip, drop of water splashing on the wooden floor. Shit, she thought, not another leak.

The building had been built in 1947. It was sturdy but like all old buildings it was in need of repairs.

Julia's ears followed the raindrop sounds and her eyes scanned the ceiling until she spotted a puddle of water that had splashed on the floor from a hole in one of the windows. She noticed that the hole in the glass was round, in fact, a perfect circle, like the lid of a coffee tin. How unusual, she commented, and decided she'd better close it up. Cutting a piece from cardboard to fill the gap served as a temporary fix but Julia wondered why old windows cracked in such a strange way. Oh well, at least I stopped the rain from coming in some more.

At 7:30 am the breakfast trays arrived. Mrs. Beauregard placed the Demisco's trays on their respective bedside tables and assumed they were in the bathroom. When she returned at 9:30am the trays were still there untouched. Since they were new residents she believed that they must be involved in medical tests. At least they will have a good lunch today, she reminded herself; turkey with gravy, mashed potatoes, carrots, broccoli, juice and ice cream would be served to them. Nathan had not disclosed to the Demisco's daughter that most meals were delivered to the resident's rooms. He had a rapacious appetite for money and constantly looked for ways to cut costs and increase profits. The new guests were given a variety of pleasant meals but eventually they, too, got use to Tom's peanut butter and jelly luncheon sandwiches.

Mrs. Beauregard went about her business as usual. At 9:45am Nurse Vicksburg delivered the Demisco's prescribed medications but the couple was not in their room. Odd, thought, Nurse Vicksburg, maybe they're outside walking off their breakfast. She left the pills on their bedside tables.

At lunchtime Mrs. Beauregard brought two trays of hot turkey with all the trimmings to room 125. The Demiscos were not there. She left the trays in the room and continued rolling her cart and delivering trays. When she reached the nurse's station she stopped and asked where the Demiscos were. Nurse Vicksburg, staring up at Mrs. Beauregard, answered, "Aren't they having lunch?" "No, nurse, they are not in their room," a worried Mrs. Beauregard replied. Nurse Vicksburg rose from her chair and walked briskly to room 125. All was tidy, lunch trays were covered and medications were in paper cups. Nurse Vicksburg returned to her station and called Mrs. Whitehall who in turn called Nathan.

In spite of Mrs. Whitehall's detailed report, Nathan could not believe that the Demiscos were missing. Yet, this could turn into some law suit, he reckoned. Setting up a preliminary investigation, he gathered all staff members who had been in their room, interviewed each, while Mrs. Whitehall took notes. Reaching a dead end, with his knickers getting tighter, he relented to Mrs. Whitehall's alarming plea to call 911.

At 1:00pm Roy took the call and listened to Nathan Cain's explanation of the events that lead to the Demiscos disappearance. Roy inquired, "Are you telling me, Mr. Cain, they went missing in your secured facility? How the hell does that happen? Weren't your night guards on duty or were they asleep at the switch?" Todd, hearing that comment, picked up the extension, as Nathan was shouting, "My guards are on duty 24-7, asshole." Todd interrupted, "Mr. Cain, please fill me in on you dilemma. This is Lieutenant Todd Miller, sir, we haven't met but we're here at your service. How can I help?" This approach brought Nathan down a peg as he quietly repeated the events. Todd weighed the information, thinking, here we go again; we have another enigma. "Mr. Cain, we'll be right over sir. Please assemble all the staff who may be relative to their possible missing." After hanging up, Todd stared hard at Roy, but knowing him, decided to drop the matter. Roy got the message and together they walked in silence to the cruiser.

Mrs. Whitehall showed Todd and Roy into Nathan's office. The sanctimonious Nathan Cain played the part of a very concerned relative. Mrs. Whitehall acted her role well, too, patting her tiny crocodile tears with a pink embroidered handkerchief. She gave Todd a list of the staff members to be interviewed while Nathan explained his findings which resulted in his 911call and offered his office to Todd for police business. Todd asked the question that Nathan feared the most. "Has the family been notified?" Lying like a snake, Nathan said he would, of course, take care of that. Todd's next question was just as stressful, "How long have they been residents?" "Oh, they came yesterday." And dear Rose is ninety one and Jerry is ninety. They appeared to be enjoying their say here, but... "But, what, Mr. Cain?" "Well, it takes a few weeks for new guests to assimilate; they always want to go back home." "Do they live with relatives or have their own home?" "They live at home and their daughter Ines and her husband Terry live close by." "Is it possible they could have taken a cab home, Mr. Cain?" "Anything's possible, I guess. Jerry's wheelchair is still in his room but according to his medical chart he was ambulatory." "Okay, Roy, send some task force personal to check on both houses." " Mr.Cain, I'd like to start with Mrs. Beauregard." Mrs. Whitehall left to fetch her.

Chapter 44

Todd listened patiently as the employees gave their time frame of events. Mrs. Whitehall escorted Reno into Nathan's office last. Todd began, "According to your report there were no sleep noises in the Demisco's room at 3:20am. What do you mean by sleep noises?"

Reno answered, "Night guard duty is a boring, uneventful, and if I may say so, solitary work, so I developed a little on the job recreation, Lieutenant. I amuse myself on my rounds by checking each room. I open the resident's door shine my flashlight in to make sure all is well. I also listen for breathing. This little task keeps me alert; it's quite lonely in these dimly lighted corridors at night. It brightens things up for me and I feel as though I'm accomplishing something, you know, helping out. Occasionally, I get the shit scared out of me when a resident taps me on the shoulder asking for help to find his room. We call them night wanderers. They roam aimlessly in the hallways unless we guide them back to their rooms."

"Okay, okay, Reno, that's a very good technique you developed. Now, when you heard no sleep noises in the Demisco's room, why didn't you go in and investigate?" "Well, Lieutenant, you can see I'm a man of large proportions. I took a step forward to enter the room but Sally called me saying dinner was being served. I was really lightheaded from hunger. Food is a priority for a man of my size and I could just smell those dumplings in browns gravy and weiner schnitzel Sally whipped up."

Roy was about to ask Reno how much he weighed but thought better of it. Todd thought to himself, Reno doesn't know how lucky he was; the ferryman was most likely on the other side of the door. Had he gone in he most likely would have gone missing along with the Demiscos. Todd asked Reno, "Have you anything else to add that may be of help, Reno?" "No, sir," but as he got up to leave he mentioned that the dumplings and schnitzel were delicious.

Mrs. Whitehall accompanied by Julia McPherson returned to the office, "Lieutenant," Mrs. Whitehall announced in her cool but excited voice, "Julia is head of our maintenance department, she just informed me of something that might be of interest to you, go ahead, Julia, tell the Lieutenant." "Sir, this morning I temporarily repaired a broken window pane down in my maintenance room." Red flags went off in Todd's head. "Julia, please take us to that location."

Julia removed the cardboard; all stared at the perfect circle. Mrs. Whitehall said jokingly, "why, only a mouse could get through that hole." Todd and Roy looked at each other in silent agreement, shaking their heads up and down. "You're right, ma'am, however, a hand could easily slip through that hole, unlatch the lock and bingo- his entry way!" declared Todd. "Roy, see that workbench over there, put it under the window. "Right sir." Todd climbed up on the bench and peered out. He saw a single black milk crate under the window. "That's it, Roy, the ferryman entered through the window and exited through a door with the Demiscos. Ten to one he hid his truck behind the dumpster in the back."

Nathan joined the maintenance room group and Todd briefed him on the latest information. Todd further explained to Mrs. Whitehall, Julia and Nathan that the hole was cut by a glass cutter. Julia interrupted, "I remember sir, that I swept up the pieces of glass and put them in that waste paper basket," pointing to the brown basket beside her desk. Roy fetched the basket, peeked in and left it in place for forensics.

Todd outlined the sequence of events the forensic team would follow in the maintenance room, the stairwell and in the Demisco's room for Nathan and assured him there would be 24-7 police protection at the home. He and Roy shook hands with Nathan and Mrs.Whitehall and left the building. Driving out of the front parking lot, Todd asked Roy, "How 'bout we go to Jack's for lunch before I fill in the Chief? You know that coffee pot holding gossiper would never forgive us if we didn't give him this juicy morsel."

Chapter 45

As Jack spread the word about the latest disappearances the already disturbed village became a community of soundless chaos. The Demisco vanishings was the final salvo that most villagers could abide. Those who could leave did. Others stayed close to home; buttoned up. Businesses closed well before sun set. A sinister fear mushroomed in every direction. Friends began to shy away from each other. An unexplained phobia baffled human understanding. It was as if a madman, in sound body, was among them. Who would be next? To know that two sweet elderly people could vanish from a secured nursing facility was unthinkable. The harmonious unity of this friendly, hardworking fishing village was severed; the beast ruled.

The unusually quiet Main Street hosted practically empty busses, a few cabs and police cruisers drove their routes. It reminded one of an old deserted Hollywood movie lot. Montaukers were strong willed, stoic and staunch fighters. Yet their dauntless spirit of resolution was being challenged inexplicably almost on a weekly basis. It was a conflict which did not determine who is right but who would be left.

A morose Sergeant Roy Thompson was reading the forensic reports in the Control Center, muttering to himself and shaking his head back and forth, when he noticed one item that aroused his attention. Forensic had put the broken glass pieces together and refit it into the pane. It was a perfect match, however, as expected, no prints were found. Roy struggled again with the fact that there was an absence of evidence.

As if he were giving an oral dissertation to his peers, Roy, with his seemingly limited vocabulary, began to pontificate. "Where the hell does he ferry them? They just disappear without a speck of a crumb. Since there are no indications of a crime we have to categorize each as a low level missing person's case by law except for Hotchkiss. If this isn't insensible and ludicrous I don't know what is. There is no consideration for the missing people because we have to stick to the law. It's a wonder that anybody gets convicted. This is an epidemic of pure insanity; nine persons disappear and one dead officer. It's just brain spattering. What a waste of all that beautiful life."

Todd was spellbound listening to Roy, who evidently didn't know he was talking out loud. "Where in hell did you come up with "an epidemic of pure insanity", Roy?" "Oh that? My Mom would yell that at us kids whenever we acted up. It's one of those Irish sayings, you know," Roy answered embarrassingly. "Hey, Roy it's okay. This case is progressing. Look, we got him off his turf, right? He's now starting to expose himself like never before. Force equals pressure, Roy. We're drawing him out in the open, not like the usual psycho who often hides. Have faith, Roy, we'll neutralize him soon. This whole apocalypse he created is about to collapse. And I have a peculiar feeling or call it intuition Roy; it's going to happen soon." Todd could see the change in Roy's expression as he gave him the pep talk. "Don't marry your case, Roy. Don't make commitments, just stick to the facts. Keep it non-personal." "Thanks, boss, I know I get too into things." "Right," Todd agreed. "I'm in the mood for a good cup of coffee Roy, let's head over to Jack's." I'll have to explain to Roy how not to marry your case, Todd reminded himself.

Chapter 46

Entering the helm, Cary greeted Calvin with her usual "Good Morning, Cal," but added apprehensively, "there's a nasty nor'easter heading our way. Do you really think going out today is the right move?" Calvin look up from his chart, "Cary, this down easter was built especially for this type of rough weather. The season's coming to a close, you know. Water temperature is lowering, bait is on the move, heading south and soon our fish will be leaving. You know the scenario Cary, they make their final move."

Cary asked reluctantly, "Where to, Captain?" "Set course for Jennie's Horn. My dragger friends said it was boiling with blue fin tuna. Keep the VHF on the weather station and monitor the updates. I expect we can get a half day of fishing, better than nothing. When the blow shows up, we'll make for port. Now, don't let your heart be troubled, mate, there ain't nothing this boat can't handle. Wake me when we're five miles from the Horn."

The Shark Killer's engines were all warmed up and ready for her run out to the Horn. Cary waited until Calvin gave her the go sign. As soon as she saw his thumbs up signal she engaged the throttle and the 'shark' was off on another hunt. As Cary steered her out of the harbor, she noticed the barometer was dropping. Shit, she thought, I never question his judgment but I hope he knows what he's doing. The weather reports insist this is not just a regular storm but an all out blow. It's not like Calvin to be careless. He is definitely strange these days. His secluded world has become even narrower. Damn, I have to inch in between the cracks. Maybe the ugliness of it all has got to him. He won't even talk about it with me. He sleeps going out and coming back now. What the hell is he up to at nighttime?

Cary, the seasoned salt that she was, could see the storm clouds; those birds of the air, that never slept, starting to set up for trouble. Right now it's a lady's wind, she knew, but in eight or nine hours the angry edge of the storm swells would show up. Oh well, he's Captain, I'm mate. I follow orders doing what I'm told. He's never been wrong except for that damn shark tournament shit. Losing by just seven pound was a damn burn to his confidence. Calvin's not the same Calvin I used to know; seems to have taken on a dark side, like a new identity that I'm surer in hell not in harmony with. That's it; his inharmonious harmony has confounded me. He used to raise the devil with me and that was fine 'cause I knew where he was coming from. Now he's just a roughhouse of unpredictability. One minute he's here for me, the next he's a sidewinder. How in hell can I deal with these unexpected changes? He's a tyrant. The pleasures we have shared are gone. Is this the downward slope of a man as he ages? Or is he concealing something dark and deep from me? His moods go back and forth, he watches everything I do. He's become a watchman on patrol. What the hell is all this subterfuge? I don't want to lose my man but I really think I've already lost him.

Cary clicked on the speaker. "Captain, sir, we're five miles to Jennie's Horn. Looks like you're right, Captain, we'll get in a couple of good hours of fishing before the swells show up. Cary put the Shark Killer on auto pilot, thinking, it would be best to get some ice now before we get fishing. She had to go down to the big freezer since the small ice maker was on the blink.

She opened the large cold stainless steel door, the light went on. She began to fill her container with ice.

Her eyes drifted and became transfixed on an object in the freezer. Startled with fear and not willing to accept what she saw, she staggered backwards with the image of a hand wearing a gold wedding band in her mind. The misty freezer light reflecting off the cold blue ice gave the hand a bizarre violet afterglow. Cary was about to blackout when suddenly, from somewhere above her, came a roaring terrifying sound. It was Calvin, towering over her, screeching, "woman, why are you in this freezer?" Forcing her eyes away from the hand and looking up at him, she heard herself mutter, "I needed ice for our drinks." Calvin stepped between Cary and the frozen hand, "I just got in some fresh squid the tuna love it. It freezes up real good. Now take your ice and get us to the Horn."

Shaken with terror, Cary returned to the safety of the helm. She repeated the Lord's Prayer silently, over and over and over again.

Cary sensed she was no longer on her familiar boat but rather floating on the water on an alien ship. It was as if she was caught in a creature's lair; the kind of space we all fear and abhor. The thought of that hand was so gruesome but at the same time brought tears to her eyes. Who the hell was this man turned beast? How could he use people for bait? The evil of her discovery was so overwhelming; she feared she couldn't remain steady for long,

The loathsome weight she endured escaped her for a brief second as she glanced down at her orca tooth. No matter how insidious this catastrophe the tooth would defend her. It wasn't a matter of kill or be, killed, she reasoned, it was a circumstance of faith. She knew she must trust in the wisdom of the lord of the tooth.

While Calvin attended to his fishing tasks, Cary brought the boat to the dock. They secured the craft. Cary departed in silence. She managed to get to her truck. In a state of calm panic, she turned on the engine, put the gear into drive and sped away. He watched from the helm, assumed she was on her way to the police and knew he had to exercise his plans in a hurry.

The nor'easter was traveling at a faster speed that predicted and before long the sea would be in a turbulence that would be to Calvin's disadvantage. Cary was out of sight; she had seen him staring at her from her rear view mirror. When she could no longer recognize his form, she hit the brake and shaking so, her boot slapping the pedal and her hands almost unable to handle the wheel safely, she pulled off to the side of the road.

Coming to a full stop, she turned the engine off and leaned her head back to rest. To have turned human life into chum, she whispered, is the most diabolical cruel scheme a man could come up with. This abhorrent act is even lower than cannibalism. Oh, the Lord will thrust him into those fires that shall never be quenched. What can I do to save the precious treasure of life before he acts again? Cary broke down crying herself dry. Her orca tooth seemed to have lost its brilliant shine. It must be trying to tell me something, she thought. She sat up slowly, regained the needed control and pulled back on the road. It was Sunday. She knew where to go. The rain began pelting her windows; the wipers swung furiously back and forth.

Chapter 47

Cary walked through the door and over to Todd's counter, her heart pounding her body taut. Trying to catch her breath, she stuttered, crying, "Oh God, oh God, oh, Calvin's the one you're searching for. I saw the horrible thing in his freezer and.........She dropped her head into her hands to catch the tears as they fell on the counter top. "Cary, dear, get a hold of yourself, what did you see in the freezer? Take a deep breath dear." Todd got a bottle of water from his frig and handed it to her, trying to coax Cary to drink a little. She swallowed a few sips. A chill flowed through her aching body, her mouth was so dry, her throat on fire. It felt as if a red hot poker was in her belly. She knew she was going to be sick. Holding her stomach and bending over alerted Todd. He ran for the waste basket as Cary fell to her knees and filled the basket a quarter of the way up; gagging on the remains in her mouth. Her eyes were wet and bloodshot. Trembling, she tried to sip the shot of light rum that Todd urged her to drink. He guided her gently over to his desk chair where she sank into it like a rag doll. Disgusted with her actions, she whispered her apologies.

Todd kneeling beside her asked again, "Cary, what was it you saw in Calvin's freezer that upset you so?" "Todd, it was so appalling, so ghastly that I don't want to think about it." Todd had his suspicions about what Cary would reveal. Once more he probed, "Cary, my dear, what is the, it?" Cary refilled the shot glass, took a hard gulp and held out her open hand. "It was a hand buried under the loose ice. It had a gold wedding band on the finger." Her next words were shouted, "THE MONSTER HAD A HAND FROZEN IN THE ICE." She took a small sip of the light rum and continued calmly and softly, 'He tried to put me off, said something about just getting fresh squid, he must think I'm a fool." "Maybe that's what kept you alive, Cary." "Maybe so, Todd, but I believe the ocra's tooth protected me." She pulled it up over her jacket. Once again the tooth glowed.

Todd continued to question Cary as easy going as possible. Her fear seemed to have waned but her grief and rage resonated silently. "Cary does Calvin own a

Glock pistol?" "Yes, Todd, he has two Glock pistols, I carry one since the disappearances."

That's exactly the Hotchkiss connection, Todd figured and now he knew where he ferried the bodies. Oh, Lord, he kept them in his freezer until he ground them up for bait, right there on his boat. The dementia of his mind is infinite.

"Cary, there's a substantial reward to which you're entitled; you cracked this case, it's yours." "My, oh my Todd, I had no idea. But Todd, I am "tired and weary laden" as my Mother used to say. Just please get me home." "Sure thing Cary, I'll just lock up."

As they pulled up to Cary's cottage, Todd's cell rang. "Yes, Roy, what's up?" "You're not going to believe this, Todd, a one Captain Calvin Cain owns a Glock." "Roy, in fact, he purchased two." "Shit, Todd, how the hell did you know? I just got this info not five minutes ago." "That's not important now, buddy, I'll fill you in later. For now get the entire task force down to Calvin's dock. "I'm already on my way. Roger that Todd."

Cary stepped wearily out of the truck, thanked Todd and told him to be careful. "You're no match for him; please wait for your boys to show up." "Thanks.

Cary, I have no intentions of going near him 'til I see the task force." She knew Todd was no cocky kid. He had a family for which he was responsible. She turned and started down her wet stone walkway, clutching the bottle of light rum. The pouring rain was warm for this time of year. Actually, it is, refreshing, thought Cary. Oh, that it would wash away my sea of despair, to God, be the glory, she prayed.

Chapter 48

The storm was becoming rapidly worse. Calvin throttled up the "Shark Killer II". She responded, cutting smartly through the harbor's agitated waters. It was nearly the close of day when the nor'easter brought its dark and angry clouds. The dusk of impending night was upon Calvin. Not wanting to call attention to himself, he didn't turn on his running lights and used the intermittent whitish blue lightning to help guide his boat out through the jetty. He piloted passed the well known restaurant and its parking lot and saw the red flashing police lights heading into the lot. One lone truck was already parked there with its high beams on. Its intense light shone from the western jetty to the eastern jetty as if to set up a light barrier to thwart his progress.

Todd saw the task force arrive from the front seat of his truck. Too late, he knew. Once the team realized Calvin had left his boat slip, they drove to the lot. It's all in the timing, Todd knew. Calvin happened to be a few paces ahead of them. Todd watched as the boat sliced through the pelting blowing rain of his headlights. He could see that every time the boat's bow smashed through an on coming wave spray shot up and enveloped the vessel like some sort of fiendish ghost craft. Lightning would illuminate the boat again and the severe spray would conceal her once more within the walls of the furious water.

As Roy pulled up next to Todd, the "Shark Killer II" had escaped the harbor and began her voyage through the turbulent gale, obscured by the suit of night and towering waves. Roy jumped into Todd's truck. "Well, that's that," he sighed, as he studied the sheets of rainwater now turned red from the flashing police lights. "Roy, now just how far do you think he's going to get in this storm?" "Yeah, you're right, Todd, he's going to have one hell of a job navigating through this." "You know Roy, he has GPS and the down easter was purposely built to handle this type of storm. My guess, he's either heading north or south, he'll hug the coastline which will cut some of the thrust out of the wave action and wind. You know something Roy, in these gale force winds and conditions we can't send up helicopters and Coast Guard sent their forty seven foot boat to D. C. for one of the golden anniversaries. That leaves them with their twenty eight footer, no way will they attempt to use it." "Only a madman would go out in this," Roy interjected. "Thank you, Roy, that's what we've been dealing with." "Do you think he'll try to double back, you know wait us out?" "Trust me Roy, not that guy, he has a plan which he means to accomplish." "Hey, Todd, what will happen if we do catch him?" "Don't even think about it, Roy. Go home and get some rest Roy, I'm going home to Jamie and the kids. It's been one hell of a day. Night buddy." As they clicked off their flashers, the red sheets of water appeared white, through the high beam lights. When the last car left the pouring rain took on the new color of midnight black.

Chapter 49

Storms do speak, Calvin knew. The wind howls in different keys, the rain pelts its patter against the windows and about the cabin creating a chorus of particular tones. The waves thunder against the bow with a smashing drum like resonance. On coming rushing white water plays its own prologue of groans and shrieking cries as it washes down the forward deck, spilling and swooshing over the sides. Every so often, the lightning cracks a warning shot; its sound waves ricocheting. Calvin was accustomed to these orchestral sounds since he spent most of his life on the sea. He found a unique comfort from Mother Nature's reverberations even in dangerous times like this.

All was right with his ship; the engine was working normally. Her builders had molded her for the aggressive, violent sea. Calvin drew strength from her power over the waves; he was one with his "Shark Killer II". Now it was all in the timing. He'd throttle down as he entered a downward slope and throttle up as he reached the crest. It was a game of give and take and the player that he was remained standing, clutching the stainless steel wheel bracing himself against the seat and staring ahead and judging each on rushing wave.

The gale was no doubt out to get him, he figured, and, although, he wasn't in fear of dying, he sure didn't want to end up in the ocean as chum. He felt invincible and eternal. As a depraved grin broke across his face, a slash of bright lightning illuminated his sinister fashioned smile causing him to resemble a gargoyle.

He began laughing and his laughter continued to almost a level of hysteria. Entertaining himself, he said a loud, "Hi, I'm Sean O'Reilly, holding out his outstretched hand, "who ever grabbed that hand was dead. Like little germs, I crushed them, chopped them up for bait and was willing to wait to catch my treasured trophy."

Swaying with the rolls, losing his footing often and squinting with his one eye as he tried to see through the milky swells, he thought of his brother. "You're right, Nathan," remembering what his brother had said, "It's all about the money; you fuck them, they fuck you. Brother, you are so right, just play the gray zone."

The next huge wave pounded over the bow; Calvin braced himself for the impact that didn't come. "Shark Killer II" once again sliced it in two. "That's my girl, that's my girl; rid me of those bastards out there like that meddling bitch Cary. I should've clubbed her in the freezer but there was an aura around her like some sort of veil of protection. Funny, it held me back, like no harm could touch her; divine intervention or was it goodness championing over evil? I should turn the boat around and get all three of them; Cary, Nathan and that fat belly Tom. They're a malignant curse." Roaring in a heinous, horrifying kind of laughter, his boat joined in, pulsating dangerously with her mad master.

"How clever, of me to have, eluded capture! What the police didn't know was that I had a police scanner tuned to their task force frequency. As I cruised passed them when they were in the parking lot they must have been beside themselves. The single truck with those high beams must have been their top gun, Todd." Again, Calvin laughed a long, eerie cackle.

He took another GPS reading. The currents had moved him quite a bit off course. He eased the boat to port watching the road map again become aligned to the correct coordinates. Another compass reading assured him he was back on course.

In a flash he was back to his thoughts, reflecting on his pious bastard brother sitting high up in his oval oak office in his three piece suit. "You smug shit," he yelled, "you're no better than me; you just play a different tune. You're ripping off the government and all the Medicaid money. You're stealing from residents and their families. Why you even sent the dead to an ocean grave. I outsmarted you, brother, both Mrs. F. and Mrs. Di Palma wound up in my chum bucket; no use in wasting good bait in the canyon."

Jesus, let me sit in hell with my brother, maybe we could talk and find out what went wrong. We'll have all eternity to discuss the pros and cons. What happened to the morality our parents taught us? We were pure once. Where did it go? Calvin grabbed his thermos and took a long drink of hot black coffee to keep pumped up.

There was no mistaking it. He was getting closer to the Cape May Inlet. Too bad I had to do this, he thought. Losing Montauk's great fishing grounds and all those thrills is going to hurt. It was either this or a cell. Had to empty out my bank account fast; one hundred and forty eight thousand, all in small bills. I'll scuttle the boat and make off for New Orleans. Maybe, I'll be a shrimp boat Captain, why not, it's good money? Lay low for awhile, 'til the heat is off. That bitch made me change my life style, oh well, she was a good mate.

Chapter 50

He entered the Cape May Inlet searching for the red markers to guide him into safe harbor but even though it was calmer the wave sets of six to seven feet continued to do battle with the bow. The wind had decreased a noticeable few notches and the barometer was on the rise indicating a sure sign that the weather would improve. Nevertheless, he had to find those red markers. He turned on his navigational lights and switched on his powerful bow beams. As Calvin turned starboard he caught sight of the rock jetties peeking out of the tops of the waves. He knew this was not good; the current had taken him too close to the shoreline. Realizing that he was on the left side of the markers, he turned hard port. "Shark Killer II" obeyed, swerving to the left, slicing eagerly through the swells. Suddenly, the sky was lighted by billions of candlepower, their arrows of lightning exploding everywhere, their cobalt blue and white flashes flicking over the mountains of water. With alarming concern, Calvin turned port side, to see only a massive thirty foot wall of green water thundering toward him. At the very top of the rogue wave was angry, boiling white water. As the roaring wave drew closer the top of its crest began to spill over. Picking up speed as it flowed down the wall created an enormous white avalanche that pushed and crushed the boat into the barrier of rock jetties. The keel was ripped to shreds, the fuel tank was pierced, the electrical system sparks meshed with the escaping fuel causing a massive explosion. The fiery orange and red ball rose high into the atmosphere forming a mushroom cloud.

The thunderous percussion of the explosion alarmed the people at the nearby marina. They contacted the local authorities. It was anyone's guess; was it a small plane or a boat? Rescue and recovery efforts were delayed until the storm abated. It was not until first light that the search could begin in earnest.

From the recovered wreckage they could tell that it was most definitely a boat. Was it, in fact, the boat that had left Montauk the previous evening, was still undetermined until one of the firemen walked into the makeshift control center tent holding an orange ring buoy. The bold black lettering on the flotation device read SHARK KILLER, II, MONTAUK, N.Y.

Chief Rawlins of the New Jersey Police was put directly through to Chief Becker. Rawlins informed Becker the orange ring buoy confirmed it was indeed the "Shark Killer II". He further indicated the explosion demolished most of the boat; they were recovering bits and pieces, no body parts. Rawlins presumed Calvin Cain was now traveling with the fish. Chief Becker thought how ironic the bait master himself wound up as chum; good prevailed over evil. The executioner was dealt his fair punishment, he explained to Rawlins who promised to call with any further developments. They both hung up smiling.

Todd and Roy were closing down the Control Center when their Chief walked in with the good news. Chief Becker studied Todd's ferryman chart for a moment and remarked, "He's done his last ferrying." All three shook their heads in agreement.

EPILOGUE I

It was one month later. Roy was back to his usual routine except for the skull found on the beach in Cape May, New Jersey. Roy faxed Calvin Cain's dental records to Chief Rawlins' forensic team. The skull, identified as belonging to one Calvin Cain, was shipped by helicopter to East Hampton Police Headquarters. Upon arrival Roy secured the stainless steel case in the evidence room, wrote his last report and filed it under D for Disappearance. Roy informed Todd who in turn passed the information along to Jack. Once again the news spread throughout the humming hamlet. Roy's final task was to notify Nathan Cain and to instruct him to procure his brother's remains. An annoyed and displeased Nathan decided immediately that he would make arrangements to have the repugnant skull tossed into the same location where two of his former residents now resided.

EPILOGUE II

It was New Year's Day; temperatures were hovering at thirty one degrees at 6:30 in the morning. A light snow was falling. Cary stepped out of her truck and walked the familiar fifteen paces to the edge of the slip that once berthed "Shark Killer II". The name plate that had once identified the boat and her Captain was removed. Cary unwrapped the rose, freeing it from the green tissue paper. She spoke in a soft voice, "I am mating for Captain Mark on the "Heavenly Father II". He lost his wife last year. We went to a New Year's Eve party last night. He's sleeping off his Dalwinnie malt on the rocks." Cary tossed the rose into the middle of the slip and watched it sail out into the harbor as the sea breezes caused the petals to appear to be waving. The snow was falling harder; it was time to get back. "I'll fix up a fire and make Captain Mark's breakfast," she said, and walked back to her truck.

EPILOGUE III

Spring arrived and with it a renewal of the spirit of the villagers. The human storm that shattered so many lives had passed. It was a time to reflect on one's grace and faith. For generations the people of Montauk played with the cards they were dealt; no matter the deal. Their appreciation and understanding of their surroundings and of humankind allowed them to continue. Montauk's magic returned; paradise was restored and inhabited by the deserving survivors.

Printed in the United States
100315LV00004B/235/A